Short Stories for the Fireside

Sitting near the hearth now, on my old worn sofa; I remember early in my life that special feeling I often had while reading with only the light from the fireplace to see by. Of course we had electricity, but the smell from the oak logs burning brightly; well…it just made winter feel more special.

And with the fire flickering next to me now, I have put together several stories which I have created that remind me of those winter evenings; stories that seem to me were meant to be read by firelight.

To that end, I give you stories that may make you laugh, may make you cry, or perhaps become sad… stories that I hope you will remember long after you read them.

Joseph L. Rose

Mondragone, Italy

This book is dedicated to my wife…

Giovanna

Starlight Sequel: Miss Mary

It's been two whole year since we had won that trophy, still sitting here in our school library; on the counter next to the librarian's desk. Zeke said that maybe we could get to keep it, but I kind of doubted that. Miss Lillie had told us that it was an annual award, given to the winning team each year. We used to practice every day after classes, and sometimes before classes began. But when Miss Lillie died two months ago, on the 2nd day of February; we stopped. With no coach, it seemed pointless even to practice anymore.

Miss Mary came to town right after that, just before Easter, on a bright spring morning. She was hired as the new account for our orphanage and we were told that she was also taking the position of acting Mayor until the next election. No one mentioned a new coach for our team, and to tell you the truth; we had learned many times over never to expect much. We knew our position in life, "our being special"; as Miss Lillie would say.

'Hey Joe," came a voice from behind me that I knew very well. "Hi Betty," I replied, not even having to look back. "Don't look so glum," she said, "I have some good news for us. Miss Mary is going to coach our team." "No way," Zeke said, just now walking up to our table in the school cafeteria. "I overheard Mrs. Hopkins tell the school counselor this morning in the front office," Betty said. "And," she continued, "I heard her say that she was going to have to adjust her hours, but now since she had our financial ledgers up to date again; she would have the extra time." "She does seem like a nice lady," Zeke offered, then said, "I hope she is," as he crossed his fingers.

"Hi kids," said Miss Mary, now walking up to our table; the continued, "I know that you all have a darn good underground communications system here, so I guess you all have heard that I'm going to be your new table tennis coach. Is this your entire team?" she asked. I told her that Mark and Andy were outside playing basketball, but probably would be in soon because we all have the next class together. "You're all senior's this year, am I right? She asked even though I thought she already knew the answer. "Yes, Miss Mary," Zeke told her. "Great, because I have some good news for you, that is; if you guys are still interested in playing table tennis for the school this year," she said, then added, "I'll be in the library this afternoon at three o'clock. Please pass out these flyers during the next period, and don't worry; I have already gotten permission from your teacher. See you all later!" then she turned and walked off towards the teacher's lounge. Betty picked up one of the flyers, then she read aloud: "Starlight Orphanage & School. This afternoon will be a meeting for our Starlight Table Tennis Team. Everyone interested in playing for our school is invited to attend. No prior experience necessary." It was signed, Miss Mary Cantrell.

"What do you think Joe, will it break up our team?" Zeke asked. I looked at the flyer, and then saw that Betty was staring at me; and said, "Listen, we have to think of our school too; we need replacements once we have graduated. I would like to think that we can help new players learn the game. Like Miss Lillie taught us, and what we have learned from experience in competition; it takes knowledge and quick thinking on your feet while playing." "We should make you our team Captain," Zeke said. "No, definitely not!" I replied, and added, "If anyone should be our team captain, it should be Mark. And if we do get a chance to select a team captain, my choice would be for two co-captains: Mark and Betty." "Good idea," I'll second that; now let's pass these leaflets around." Zeke said.

Mark and Andy just walked up and Zeke got them up to speed about Miss Mary. Mark said that he was just glad that we got a team going again this year. Then he looked right at Zeke, and said, "We do need new players joining us, or Starlight will not have any sports whatsoever for us kids to play." "Yeah, I know," replied Zeke, "but I can't help thinking that we are the team, just the five of us…it's been like that for seven years now, ever since the fifth grade." "Yeah, I see what you mean," answered Mark, and then added, "But what a way to meet new girls." We started to laugh, then looked over at Betty. She just stuck her tongue out at us and said, "Let's go to class boys!"

The clock on the wall above the door read 3:00 o'clock exactly when Miss Mary entered the room. She was carrying a table tennis paddle, a ping pong ball used for playing table tennis, and a notepad. She gave the notepad to Betty and asked that everyone please print their first and last name, the grade there are in, and there homeroom teacher's name. While we were passing the notepad around, she asked if anyone had every played competition table tennis. Only the five of us had raised our hands. "That's okay," she said, "we have all to begin somewhere, and somewhere is right here, right now. You all have played ping pong… raise your hands if you have. Okay, so I guess I won't have to tell you what I am holding in my hands. No, I am not trying to be funny. As Joe, Mark, Zeke, Andy and Betty there in the back can assure you; table tennis is not a funny game… especially competition table tennis. The reason I keep saying "competition", is that our school only plays in competitive matches. No other school in our district plays table tennis. We play against other schools in the southern region of our state and have been doing so for the last few years."

Miss Mary paused, took a drink from her water bottle, and then walked over to the librarian's counter and pointed to the Iron Paddle Award. "It is pretty impressive and a much coveted award. Many, many schools in the southern region would love to have this back in their district. The reason it is here is because the last time we played, we won the tournament. Mark won the Singles and Betty and Joe the Doubles match. The tournament was not held last year due to tornadoes, ice storms, and rivers flooding much of the southern tier. The storms are over, the ground is dry, and the southern schools want the Iron Paddle back in there district. There is only one way they can take it back… you want to tell everyone here how that is done Mark?" "You have to win the tournament?" Mark replied.

She took the small white ping pong ball and hit it over to Tommy in the first row. Tommy caught it, and tossed it back. "Looks kind of simple, just hitting the ball; doesn't it? She asked to no one in particular. Then she took the same ball and slammed it hard over to me. I caught the ball, and guessed what she was going to say next. "In competition, that ball will be coming at you from 45 to over 75 miles an hour. It will sting, it will hurt, and yes, you can even scrape your knuckles and bleed all over the place. For a non-contact sport, we carry two large cans of Band-Aids with us to every match. And I have scheduled 12 pre-tournament matches with schools in the southern tier for this school year. Many of them are real curious on just how a bunch of "orphans" managed to win a coveted trophy as the Iron Paddle Award. And just in case you're wondering, I had to have the award appraised last week when I was balancing our books. Even though we don't own it outright, but because it is in our possession, we still have to have insurance in case of accidental damage or loss. And to tell you the truth, it actually has increased in value: it's now worth over $13,000 dollars.

She let that number sink in for a while, with everyone on the room looking at the trophy on top of the counter. "Yes, it is a very expensive trophy. And it's really a one-of-a-kind, and can only be won is through our tournament matches. I brag all the time about the trophy. And that is why Lincoln is the first team we are scheduled to play. One that thing before I let you go. Those of you who are interested please show up tomorrow at the gym with a note from the school nurse. That's a state and federal requirement, not mine. My requirement is simple: you come to learn, you come to play table tennis; and you come to play table tennis my way. Those of you who remember Miss Lillie, well, she taught me to play table tennis when I was attending this same school a few years back. We weren't allowed to complete against other schools back then, something about us not being very bright; you know what I mean. Well, times have changed, attitudes have changed; and Starlight has changed. Today will be the last time I preach in front of you. Those of you who want to play will learn how to play table tennis… the way Miss Lillie taught me…by the book. Class dismissed.

The next day as we entered the gym Miss Mary said for us to go over to the attendance table and sign ourselves in. "I see some of you have your own paddles. Please set them aside for now and remember to take them home tonight… and keep them there. She opened up a large cardboard box and took out brand new paddles, red rubber on one side and black on the other. "Betty," she called out, "what is the thickness of the rubber on your paddle?" "Two millimeters," Betty replied. "And," Miss Mary continued, "assuming that her paddle meets regulations, can anyone tell me where she got that information from? And you people in the back, please keep your hands down; this is for the new players on our team." Tommy raised his hands, and said, "probably from the book of rules." "Right, you are correct Tommy," Miss Mary continued, "and that's exactly the one thing that we will have to deal with in every single match. That's why just hitting the ball is not enough. Just out scoring your opponent, may or may not necessarily win you the match. Many tournaments have been lost because a player makes a rule violation. You have to be alert, and know the rules as well as being able to put a back spin on the ball."

She picked up the attendance log and saw that three players had not shown up for practice. Then she took out several sheets of paper from her brief case. "These are practice schedules as well as matches that are played away from Starlight. For every away match the school will require permission slips from your sponsors, or the school vice principal. I know this sounds kind of dumb for an orphanage, but the state and federal requirements insist that these be kept on file. I want you newer kids to talk to the other team players that have been here all along. Those are the ones you will want to go to for advice. They are the ones that you will practice with and practice against. They will teach you how to serve properly, for example. And what I mean by properly is what the judges at the tournament will be expecting to see from each and every one of you. Now split up, grab yourselves a paddle. Please be sure to log the number on the end of your paddle next to the number on the attendance log. That will be yours throughout the entire season, or seasons, if you want. I will only replace worn out paddles. Take it back to your room...sleep with it, whatever you want; but if you show up without a paddle...you will not play. Enough said.

We started to break up into twos, and then I saw Mark reading the side of his paddle, and I looked at mine. Mine read: 2.4 ounces. I went over to him, "What's wrong?" I asked. "Just checking," he said. "I know there is no rule on the weight of the paddle, but sometimes I like a lighter paddle and other times a much heavier one." "I'm sorry Mark," Miss Marry said, and "excuse me for overhearing your conversation. I never thought about that, but I do remember back when I was playing; I had two paddles… one heavier that the other. The light one I used for competition and the heavier one for practice." "That's what I had in mind too." Mark said. Miss Mary then picked up a paddle from the carton and said, "Listen everyone," there are enough paddles to go around, so I anyone wants to have an extra paddle, go ahead and sign for one. And you can thank Mark for that," and she just grinned.

Three weeks passed and we practiced every day. The newer players were getting better, and I found myself playing almost every day with a girl named Marcie. She and I were the same age, and soon became part of our group. Betty taught her how to put a spin on the ball, since they were both left handed; Marcie picked up on it quickly. And when she and I played, I honestly had trouble returning her ball.

The days went by quickly now, and even though we were scheduled to play Lincoln, they had trade off with Westminster due to their coach having to take an emergency leave of absence. So the every next Wednesday, we found ourselves at Westminster Academy. We never played them before but were looking forward to the opportunity. Zeke had read in our local newspaper that Westminster was third overall in standings last year. They got to play against other catholic schools not in our region due to the flooding in our southern tier. This year, however, they are back and ready to play the team that had won the Iron Paddle Award. All we knew is that we were ready to play. Normally we had to win at least six of our regional matches to qualify for the tournament, but as the last winner of the award, we didn't have to worry about winning; we were pre-qualified. So we knew even if we didn't win against Westminster, we still would be in the tournament at the end of the regular schedule. That put our minds at ease, but as Betty said, "I don't know about your guys…but I want to win."

Even though we got to keep the Iron Paddle Award at Starlight, it is taken to the tournament for all to see. Yesterday, Miss Mary mentioned something that Miss Lillie never told us, that whichever school wins the award a total of four times; get to retain it indefinitely. Then she asked us to follow her into the library where she had us sit down on the floor in front of her. She then excused herself, and walked out of the room. We just sat there, looking at each other. I looked around our group. We had a total of seven players now, with Marcie and Billy making the team. Actually, there were no tests, or examinations; just the willingness to do your best…is what Miss Mary said.

Five minutes later she returned, reached over the counter, and picked up the trophy. She looked at it for a few seconds, then finally said, "You remember that I said that it takes four tournament wins for us to keep this award here at Starlight indefinitely, right?" We all nodded our heads and then she continued, "Well, as you know, I played for Starlight in the past, and I was on the team for five years. This award had been the envy of all the schools in our region for the past twenty years. It's really not the value, it is the prestige and honor that is associated with this award. Several top table tennis players, and I mean our professionals, have attempted to win this award at one time or another. They and their schools never came close to winning four times. And I have something else that I bet you never knew. After a team wins this award their names are not only inscribed on the paddle, but their school names goes on the side of its base." She then picked up the trophy and pointed to its base. It looked like it was made from black marble and approximately ten inches square and about three inches thick. "After each win," she continued, "the winning school is engraved on one of the sides, then a photograph is taken of all the sides and given to each school in the region. This year, however, our name was engraved on the top portion of the base because there was no room left on the sides. We know that no school would have their name engraved dishonestly, we since we are a stickler to the rules; this is a tournament requirements. Betty, please pass these photographs around. There is a set for each of you. Please take five minutes to look at each one. I'll be right back."

She returned after about ten minutes, carrying a tray of drinks; and I got up to help her. "Hot chocolate for everyone," she said with a big smile on her face. "Now guys," she continued, "what did you find that I am sure was of interest to you all?" "Nothing!" Betty replied, then added, "except that Starlight was only on their once." Miss Mary just smiled again, and said "That's because the years have passed and some of the names are hard to read, but they are still there." Then she picked up a chalk eraser and a piece of white chalk. She the rubbed the eraser with the chalk until it was completely white. Then she placed the eraser along one side of the base and pressed against it. "Now look," she said, "there visible now, and there we saw "Starlight Orphanage" embedded in the marble. Then she turned the base around and did the same to the opposite side, and again; Starlight appeared. Then she said, "The names of the players are on the silver paddle above, with the Starlight team of 1964 being just above the handle and the 1967 team along the right side of the handle. And, if anyone wanted to look really close to the names, you will see my name is also included; along with Miss Lillie's." We just sat there, flabbergasted.

Zeke finally spoke up first and said, "You mean that if we win this year, it will be ours?" "It sure will," Miss Mary said, "and you had better believe that the coach of Lincoln is aware of that too. He was on the Lincoln team when I played and he is still sore that I took a match away from him. In fact, he called me the other day to wish us luck on this upcoming season. But I just think he was just being polite. So guys, now that you know the history, what do you think: do you want to keep this trophy forever, or give it back to the tournament?" 'Miss Mary," I said, "you already know the answer to that, but I just want to say that winning the trophy isn't just for our team, it's for all us who have played for Starlight; in the past as well as now." "Your absolutely right," she said, "and that is exactly what I want you all to keep in mind during ever match this year. For this is the year to not only win but to keep the trophy. And listen, I am not going to kid you, for some of our best players who are seniors will be gone after this year. At it will be our seniors, with their leadership and teaching; that will have a direct impact on us next year."

"In addition," Miss Mary continued, "I have been doing a little bit of math and I thought that you guys in particular would like to know that I have come up with a figure that would astound all the schools in our region. For you guys right here in front of me, given your previous years on the team, I have calculated the following: totaling all the matches you have played; including tournament matches, you have an aggregated total of 2,363 matches. Digging a little bit deeper, that equates to 1,960 wins and only 403 losses in five years. And I don't have to tell you that, even if I had access to the other schools statistics; that you have a regional record which is unmatched by any school in America. That is why the Iron Paddle Award is here with us today, not because you won matches during a tournament; but that you are what the tournament is all about… and that is Starlight!"

She walked around the counter and came next to a chair and sat down. She then looked over at Tommy and said, "Tommy, what is on Page 11?" "It has to do with serving," Tommy said, "and that the ball needs to be served while falling down from the server's hand." "You're right, and thank you for that response because it is almost letter perfect from the rule book. I was at your tournament two years ago, as I have been every chance I get to attend a Starlight match. Watching you play, I noticed that both Brisbane and Lincoln did exactly the opposite and was never called on it. I knew Lincoln's coach was aware of the foul because I saw him crunch his teeth every time a player tossed the ball up and hit it. Well, were not going to take that chance, for everyone will learn the rules and be prepared to be quizzed on them. Help each other out, watch each other play; and don't be afraid to criticize each other. And just to reiterate, we are still playing Miss Lillie's game; nothing has or will be changed. We play to have fun, we play to win, and we play by the book!"

We came, we saw, and we conquered; as the Roman's used to say. We took Westminster Academy by storm. They were cocky at first, and we heard them make remarks about us. You know, they way we look and talk… so did Miss Mary. The home team asked that only Doubles be played since some of their team members were ill and had to have bed rest. As long as it was agreed to by the judges, and was recognized as a regional match; Miss Mary had no objections. It was the best of seven matches and we took four in a row. It was in the last service during the last game when the Westminster team cheered us. Betty took the serve on her right side and watched as the ball hit the edge of the table and spin off to the right. I don't think I have ever seen anyone move that fast. In a split second, she reached down and smacked the ball hard. I watched as it spun like a top, eased over the net, and landed on the opposite side of the table and just sat there, spinning around and around. Mr. Johnson from our Mathematics class also attended us on our trip and brought his movie camera. He had the entire match on film, especially that incredible shot. It was hard to explain, but that ball acted just like a top being pulled with a string… just spinning and spinning. Needless to say that brought cheers from both side of the gym. And that ball, Miss Mary put it in the school's trophy case along with a photograph of Betty. Betty got to sign the ball too!

The following results of our matches are listed below, having played each team twice.

Westminster vs. Starlight	0-4, 3-4
Allentown vs. Starlight	2-4, 3-4
Starlight vs. Springdale	4-0, 4-3
Starlight vs. Lincoln	3-4, 4-2
Baxter vs. Starlight	0-4, 5-2
Clemens vs. Starlight	1-4, 3-4

We played two rounds for a total of 12 matches, and we were just one happy family. We couldn't believe that we had been so successful, but under the watchful eye of our coach; we just knew we were going to win. We were heading for the tournament, and we sure wanted to play Lincoln again since they beat us that last game with a score of 4-2. Even I saw quite a few fouls, but the judges pretended not to see them and Miss Mary just let it slide for some reason.

"Listen, you guys," Miss Mary told us one evening after dinner in our cafeteria. "Look around the room," she said, "I want you to look at each other. Nothing has changed, except that maybe you were able to win a few games of table tennis. Sure, I know you're on a high now, full of excitement; ready to conquer the world. You won a few games and are entitled to complete in the upcoming tournament. Now is the time to look in the mirror." She took a mirror out of her purse and handed it to Tommy. "Tommy," she said, "Please look in the mirror. What do you see?" "I see me," he responded. "And Tommy," she continued, "If you can, tell me what you think I see when I look at you?" "A handsome young man, of course," replied Tommy. We all had to laugh at that, even Miss Mary. "That is exactly when I am talking about guys, you see yourselves as winners but the other teams will be looking at you in a much different way. They will be wondering how you won so many games in the regionals. They will be wondering how a small orphanage in the middle of nowhere got to be so good. And they will be wondering how a bunch of retarded kids ever made it this far. And then they will be wondering if you are good enough to keep the Iron Paddle Award."

She paused, then said, "Come, let us sit down next to each other. I am being hard on you because the world will be hard on you when you arrive in Lincoln. Joe, Betty, and the rest of you who have been there before know what I am talking about. The remarks people will make will be cruel, hurtful; and will make you angry. They will try to get under your skin so you will not play well, so you will be nervous; and hopefully screw up and make a zillion fouls." We all snickered at that remarked, but she continued. "I want to see young men and women enter with determination, with confidence, with pride, and with the knowledge that you may not be necessarily as good as your opponents, but one thing for sure, you are definitely superior to them of the rules of the game. And that, coupled with good clean table tennis play and etiquette; will bring the Iron Paddle Award home with you."

We're back home now, it's been a good two weeks since the tournament, and yes; we did get to the finals. Lincoln, as luck would have it, did manage to get to the finals too, even though Miss Mary counted three fouls they made during the match with Westminster, two fouls against Baxter, and two more during the final game that the judge didn't call. It was ironic, for it was Eric again who made the same mistake, and served out of sequence that cost him the match, and the tournament.

The Iron Paddle Award is back in our library, this time for good. And the morning Lincoln the newspaper that Eric's dad publishes, well; we don't need to go there!

PS.

We graduated from McNeal High, a subdivision and sponsor of Starlight; but are still staying on at the orphanage. Miss Mary got Betty a job as her secretary since she could type sixty-three words a minute. Zeke took Jose's place as gardener. Jose had been at Starlight since the beginning and now it was time for him to retire. Tommy still stays here, but has a job in town as a type setter at the Publishing Company. Mark found a home with a distant cousin in Kentucky and works at Wendy's as an Assistant Manager. Mark received a special grant from the state and is attending a local college. He is majoring in English. And me, well, I like to cook and Bertha needed an assistant…or so she said.

We're doing alright….

Copper Nails

We had gotten the call the first week of May. My uncle who lives in Italy, Uncle Joe, had become very ill and wanted to see my wife and me as soon as possible. None of us in our families were rich enough to just get on an airplane, so it took a couple of weeks for us to arrange sitters and get a small loan from our neighborhood bank. My wife Maria was able to get a week's vacation, but my boss; he said no. I guess it was just the way he said "no" in front of Maria and me that she told him: "Go to Hell!" as we stormed out of the office. My job as a security guard was one where you didn't earn sick or vacation time off. "You can easily get another job," Maria assured me. Then she reminded me that Uncle Joe was the last of my family. She had met him a few years back when we got married and honeymooned in Italy. We stayed at his home for three weeks while he visited friends in Rome. We promised him if he ever needed anything... just call. He's calling now.

The airplane landed in Bari and from there we took the train to Brindisi. The Brindisi train station was located in an open area and the minute we arrived it started to rain. Thankfully, we spotted a man standing

near the luggage area holding a sign that read "Jones".
We introduced ourselves and found that his name was
Guido, a close friend of our uncle. He had driven down
from Alberobello, the city famous for the trulli houses.
Uncle Joe's house was one of these, left to him by a very
trusted friend who said that these houses had been in his
family for generations. Of course we already knew this,
this is where we spent our honeymoon. And I think that
is why we were being asked to come right away.

Once on the road, Maria couldn't resist asking Guido
how long he knew by uncle, since the last time we were
here we hadn't met him. He just laughed and said that
he was with my uncle in Rome the whole time, it was his
house that my uncle was staying at. Then he went on to
explain that he was also asked to come down for this
meeting. My uncle had several things on his mind, and
since his health was failing; he wanted to see us as soon
as possible. "Maria," he asked, "do you still write from
time to time?" "Yes, of course," she replied. "Good",
he responded, the said, "because I have a lap top with
disks available for your use. I will tell you now that one
of the topics for discussion will be a book that he wants
to write, and it is a very important book. Although the
story may be a short one, it is one that goes back several
generations; and one that has been handed down from
family to family…and only to trusted members. I think
your uncle thinks that now maybe is the time to pass that
trust along." It started raining harder now and Guido

kept silent, paying attention to the wet narrow road that led towards Alberobello.

It was after midnight when we arrived and Guido dropped us off right in front of our uncle's door so we wouldn't get wet. Once inside we found my Uncle Joe sound asleep on his favorite chair. Maria put her shawl over his shoulders while I laid a blanket on his lap. Then we sat down at the kitchen table and looked around the room. Amazing how they built these homes, with the conical shaped roofs and rounded walls. There was a bottle of Grappa on the hearth over the small fireplace. It looked like the same one I gave him a few years back. I poured Maria and I each a small shot to ward off the chills from being out in the rain. In the adjacent rooms Maria found beds that had already been readied for our arrival and we soon retired. "We should talk with my uncle in the morning," Maria suggested, since he was fast asleep…snoring loudly.

We slept until noon and we surprised that Uncle Joe hadn't awakened us. We found him outside on the back patio talking with Guido, using both hands and words to express their meanings. I sort of smiled at myself…I talk that way too. Guido was the first to see us and got up and gave Maria his chair and soon found two others for him and me. Maria poured Italian coffee which apparently had just been made. I heard you two moving around in there so I made a fresh pot, Guide explained. "It smells wonderful," Maria said. Guido offered me a small shot of Grappa and I noticed that there were three bottles of Grappa on an adjacent table. "We're reserving the full one for dinner," Guido stated, then added, "No, just kidding. I brought another bottle down from Rome. I have a friend who works at the bottling plant and he brings me a bottle every now and then." "Here's too our Roman friends," I said, and belted it down. If you never had Grappa before, it's probably as close as you can get to white lighting... it's that strong!

"I want to thank you both for coming so quickly," Uncle Joe said, then continued, "Yes, it's true, my health if failing. And my doctor, whom I disagree with all the time; says that I have only a year, maybe less... maybe more...even maybe tomorrow. What does he know, huh? Right now I am feeling pretty good, thanks to Guido and his Grappa. Guido has probably told you that I want to tell you a story, right?" Maria and I nodded our heads. Uncle Joe motioned over to Guido and said, "Please get that lap top in the house." Back outside, Guido handed the computer to Maria. "A present," Uncle Joe said, "from Guido." Guido sat down and just smiled. Maria started to speak when Guido put up his hand and said, "Yes, it is a present. You see, this bald headed old man here says that he wants to tell you a story and he doesn't want you to use some broken old computer he has laying around... so, I bought you a brand new one just to shut him up." We all laughed at that, especially with his Italian accent. Maria thanked him and then asked Uncle Joe what is this all about.

Uncle Joe coughed a bit, then said, "I have a story to tell, and yes; before you ask, it is a true story which you probably won't believe. But please keep on typing on that computer and when I get to the end you can ask all the questions you want. Is that okay?" Maria and I again nodded our heads, and then Uncle Joe stood up and said, "But for now, let's please go into the house and eat. My neighbor Angela has made us a wonderful pan of lasagna and I can smell that it is ready." I looked across at Maria and she just smiled and nodded, he was right; the air did smell of lasagna. As we entered the dining area I noticed now cool it was. I didn't see a fan but when I saw the table laden with food, all I could think of was food. The antipasto looked appetizing and consisted of eggs, anchovies, marinated mushrooms, marinated black and green olives, marinated eggplant, marinated artichokes and small silvers of asparagus with prosciutto wrapped around each. There was a large platter of crusty bread and a large pitcher of cool red wine. Man, I was in heaven; and this was just the first course.

After the noon day meal, Maria helped Angela clear the table and my Uncle Joe and Guido poured small glasses of Grappa. Maria sat down and Guido threw a small handful of copper nails across the top of the table in front of me. They looked old and were extremely worn and tarnished. Maria picked one up and it broke into two pieces. "Oops," Maria said and the men just smiled at her. "No problem," Guido said, "if you were over two thousand years old you would break into pieces also. And not to worry, I wanted you to see these even though they came from the field behind this house. It is because this is one of the reasons you are here. Your uncle has a story that is as old as these copper nails and nails like these are a part of it. This house you are in also plays an important part because it was here when a man named Gordano lived here with his wife."

Guido poured himself another shot and continued, "The story begins several generations ago when Rome had its Third Legion quartered in and around his area. Lacking food and water, several Roman patrols entered villages and took what they could find. They also scoured the countryside looking for food. It was here in this small house that they discovered Gordano and his wife Maria. They gave them what they had in the kitchen, but when they found extra bags of wheat seed that Gordano had planned to use for planting in a nearby shed, they broke his leg for lying to them. They were also looking for runaway slaves, but Gordano had no slave markings on his neck or shoulders. The other times when they saw the Roman army they fled into the surrounding field's and stayed hidden until the army left. They thought the army would destroy their home but their leader said not to destroy the village; that several leaders in Rome were born in trulli hoses just like this one."

Guido paused again, then asked Uncle Joe if he wanted to continue the story, but he said no, Guido was doing a good job. Maria stopped typing then too and poured another round of Grappa. It began raining again outside and she was getting a chill. Guido leaned over to see the screen on the lap top and said, "You type fast, maybe 40 words a minute?" he asked. Maria just smiled and said, "Maybe twice that." "Oh," was Guido's response and Uncle Joe just sat there and smiled, then said, "Please continue Guido."

"Okay, now as I remember, Guido began, "It was during the same time that a slave named Spartacus began a rebellion that literally shook the entire southern region of Italy. He raised an army of more than 70,000 slaves before being taken down, one battle after another, by no less than seven legions of Roman troops. Near the end, Pompey captured 6,000 slaves who had surrendered. But fearing death, began running desperately trying to escape with their lives. Being overwhelmed, they were soon recaptured.

Starting from the small village of Capua, Pompey had each and every one of them all crucified along the Apian Way…all the way to Rome. Pompey never did find Spartacus' body. Thousands of dead slaves were buried in common graves and it was thought that he was included among those. Of course, the news traveled like wildfire throughout Italy. Gordano had met Spartacus once, no twice it was; once when he and his army of slaves were trying to escape north towards the Italian Alps. The second time was when the mountain pass was blocked by Roman troops and they had to retreat to the south again. They were attempting to flee to Sicily when Pompey caught up with them. Okay, enough of the history part. Maria, is everything okay with the computer… good, I'll continue with the story."

Angela brought fresh expresso coffee and Guido poured more Grappa. I held off on any more, I mean it was good…but too, too strong! Guido continued…

"It happened in the month of December, the following year after the Roman's had crucified the slaves along the Apian Way. They said that it was cold and rainy that winter, with the new grape vines struggling to hang on to the precious earth. Gordano was sleeping in his newly built trulli house, one of two he had constructed himself. He had no neighbors, except for Alfredo, who had a house two miles away. His houses serves as storage for his grain as well as sleeping and eating areas. He was hoping that the older house would go to his son one day, but so far he and his wife were barren with children. This was the night that God had spoken to him."

Guido noticed Maria suddenly perk up and look at me. She didn't say a word, and for me; I was getting really interested…for never in my life had I heard such as story as the one I was hearing now. Guido just smiled again, and continued…

"Now Gordano had heard of Jesus Christ and knew that he was crucified only three years earlier in Rome. Many of Jesus's followers traveled by his home last spring but only stayed a couple of days. He and Maria listened to them, but he had his vineyards to attend to. They worked too long and hard to give them up now. The night God spoke to Gordano, he only said a few words: "go forth, and bring back the nails." He had told Maria when he had heard from God the very next morning, but she just said: "tu patzo…you are nuts, you are crazy." The following few nights he didn't hear anything and was starting to believe that his wife was right. Not until the following week, early in the morning just before dawn; he was down by the creek getting fresh water when he heard a voice: "Gordano, go to the Apia, bring back my nails." He ran back to his house and woke up his wife and told her what had just happened. She said that she knew, that she had also heard the voice. Then she said, "He wants you to bring back the nails that the Roman army used to crucify the 6,000 slaves." Then she looked at her husband rather strangely and asked, "Gordano, how did you run back here so fast?" They both looked down at his leg. Instead of being crooked, it was straight again. He walked around the room, then they just grabbed one another and cried for a long, long time."

Uncle Joe had tears in his eyes. Guido didn't say a word, but poured another shot of Grappa and placed it in front of his old friend; then continued.

"The following Sunday he left his home, but not before asking Alfredo to look after his wife. Alfredo wanted to go with him, but someone had to stay and look after the small herd of sheep that they shared. He had no idea how far away Capua was, but he knew that the Apian Way would lead him there. Alfredo told him that the Roman's built the Apian Way a few years earlier. The road began in Brindisi and passed by Naples and Capua; finally ending in Rome. It took him two months to walk the distance, but he really didn't mind; his leg felt great. He told himself that he would walk to hell itself for God for what he had done for him by giving him the use of his leg back. He was just on the outskirts of Capua when he saw his first cross, still holding the decaying body of a slave. He took the cross down and pulled it several feet from the roadway by a rose bush, knowing that the ground would be soft there. Then he pulled the nails away from the hands and feet, three nails in all; and put them in his knapsack. He made a shallow grave and rolled the poor man into the soft ground and covered him with earth. Standing up, he brushed the dirt from his pants and went back onto the road. Looking up ahead, he could now see more crosses, lining both sides of the roadway…continuing on as far as the eye could see."

"Although he could see the small village of Capua, he stayed away; he had no business there. Several travelers stopped by, asking directions to Brindisi or just wanting to rest and talk about the news of the day. They had watched him take down several crosses but didn't inquire as to why. Apparently, they told themselves, someone in authority had ordered him to do this dreadful task. And even though Gordano didn't ask, several travelers gave him food to eat and water to drink. Gordano continue his work, day after day. Once on the other side of the village of Capua, he stopped to consider what to do next. His knapsack was full of nails. Just up the road he could see a Roman mile marker, a block of stones about three feet square and five feet high. He put his back against the marker facing towards the mountains. He then took four large steps and stopped.

On that very spot he dig a hole about two feet deep and buried all the nails he had gotten so far. He pushed on and near the village of Caserta he did the same, always using a mile marker as a location. And again, near the cities of Gaeta, Latina, and Albano he buried his heavy burden. From the mountain top near Albano he could see the city of Rome with its huge temples and amphitheaters. It was winter now, he thought, so it must be a year now that I have been on the road."

Angela came into the room, excused herself, and asked what they would like for dinner. No one had realized how late it was getting, and Maria stopped typing. She went over to Uncle Joe and held his hands. "You need rest, and my fingers need to squeeze tomatoes for the sauce for dinner." She smiled and poured a shot of Grappa. And just when I thought she had poured it for Uncle Joe, she belted it down herself. "You realize Uncle Joe," she began, "that is one hell of a story I am typing, and you are telling me that it is true; then I can't wait to hear the ending." She kissed him on the forehead and followed Angela out to the kitchen.

That evening Uncle Joe surprised us by putting on his coat and picking up his cane, then saying, "Let's go!" We walked through the streets of his small village admiring the different styles of trulli homes. We stopped from time to time to say hello to his friends, or to admire a church.   We stopped at a bar which belonged to Pasquale and we sat outside in the cool night air. The moon was high and it must have been nearing midnight when we finished off the last of Pasquale's Grappa and headed home. It was just like at home at Mikes' Bar & Grill, drinking shots and chasing them down with beer. Only this was Italian style…Grappa followed by Peroni beer.

The next morning Maria found us already outside having coffee and sat down with her lap top.   She smiled at Guido and simply said, "Pronto." Guido continued…

"Gordano found a job with a blacksmith just inside the gates of Rome. He had no interest in going into the city itself, not after what he had just been through with the poor slaves that the Roman's had killed. The only pay he wanted was the small cart that he had seen inside the blacksmith's shop. He agreed to the man's offer: he would work until spring, when the roses would blossom, and the cart would be his. Provided, of course, that he take no days off, eat his meals inside the shop, and start work at sunrise and not stop until moonrise. All through the winter Gordano worked hard each day. And it was just after the winter's thaw; he was released from his bond. The blacksmith was pleased with his work and although he regretted doing so, early in the month of

February, the cart was his. He started his return the very next day and reached Capua in good time, although the days were long and the road in bad need of repair. He had no trouble finding his caches, remembering the four steps from each marker; and soon had all of them inside his cart. And it was on a rainy evening that he saw smoke coming out of the chimney from his own house… he was home."

My wife stopped, looked at Uncle Joe, and then just smiled and said, "Okay, love the story so far, but this can't be the end, can it?" Both Guido and Uncle Joe had to laugh at that remark. "No," Uncle Joe said with a smile on his face. He looked at Guido then. Then Guido picked up a fresh bottle of Grappa and said, "You might need this for the ending." We drank and Guido poured us another. "He's not kidding," Uncle Joe remarked, and belted down his own drink. Guido continued…

"Maria had dug a hole in the floor of each of his houses. She had no idea how big each hole should be so she dug them one meter square and one and a half meters deep. When Gordano asked her why inside the houses, she had no answer; she just assumed that was where he wanted them. And, she told them, I thought that 6,000 slaves would account for a lot of nails. They set to the task of unloading the nails and placing them in each hole. It was Maria that was astonished to find that the nails filled the holes, all of them; with little room to spare. Then the put a layer of dirt and used small stones to flatten the surface. Lastly, they laid straw over the ground. The job being done, Gordano just waited for God to talk to him again. And he waited."

"Gordano and Maria eventually had a son, Michael, who grew to the age of fifteen when they knew it was time to tell him about the nails. And it was during those growing years that he and Maria found their two houses were now part of a village. Gordano, although a small man of no importance, held a deed to the properties to the east and west of him. The major of Brindisi knew of this and agreed to build him five houses if he would give him the remaining land in which to build and sell more houses. He agreed and when his five houses were built, he rented three of them; the other two he kept to store wine and grain. His rental income was sufficient and he and Maria now could relax and enjoy life a little more."

"It was on a Sunday morning that they woke Michael up at dawn. Then the three of them removed the straw from their kitchen floor and swept back the layer of dirt. The morning sun was just coming up over the horizon and was now shining through the doorway. The beam of light was now shinning on the floor…well, not exactly, actually the floor was shining right back. Maria swept away more dirt and the golden shimmering light became even brighter. She and Gordano were becoming afraid because the last time they had seen the nails was the night they placed them in the hole. Michael closed the door blocking out the sunlight and lit a lamp. With brushes now, they cleaned the surface very carefully. Finally, Maria got a wet cloth and removed the last bit of dirt. They just sat there, mouths wide open, and tried to explain to Michael what it was that they wanted him to see; not at what he was seeing now. The surface had become what appeared to be a solid one meter by one meter block of gold. Maria looked closer now and said, "Look Gordano, look close and you can see the outline of nails; only now they are gold and have been fused into a block."

It was my Maria who had to interject into his story, "a solid block of gold, you can't be serious; are you serious?" she asked. Guido looked at her, smiled, and right then and there she knew that he and Uncle Joe were definitely serious. Uncle Joe now took over from Guido…

"This house has tile on the floor, coving one of the holes that Maria had made. The other two houses still have dirt floors. I haven't covered them because I felt that you would have trouble believing this story. One thing I can tell you for sure is that the floor to this house does contain a block of solid gold. Guido and I are the ones who laid the tile squares on the floor, covering the gold. If you guys are ready, let's go into the next house and see what we will find."

I was ready and so was my Maria. What was troubling me was why this gold wasn't being used, why it was being kept a secret. We soon arrived next door and it didn't take long for Guido and me to sweep away the straw on the floor. I picked up a hoe and began scraping away dirt, layer by layer. Eventually, I struck metal and bent down on my knees to brush aside the dirt. Maria and Guido did the same and son we had a shiny surface. Maria held a flashlight on a specific area and used a wet cloth to wipe away any remaining dirt. "Look," she said excitingly, "you can actually see the outline of nails. They do appear to be fused together, and they appear throughout the entire surface. If we were to remove the cube you would probably see them on each side too."

I swept up the dirt while Uncle Joe and Guido placed a large area rug over the entire surface. Then they found another and laid it over the first one. Finally, Guido rolled a couple of casks and placed them directly over the hole as we left the house.

Back at Uncle Joe's patio. "How should we end this story?" he asked as he sat down again. "First of all," Maria said, "is that I am in need of another shot of Grappa... please!" We all laughed again as Guido poured Maria two shot glasses filled to the brim. It was I that spoke up next. "I'm sorry," I blurted out, "but I just got to ask, that after all these years, why is this gold still buried?" "You know from my story," Uncle Joe began, "that Gordano had a total of seven houses in the beginning. Through the years, your ancestors had increased their holdings here by buying up homes that people had vacated due to wanting to return to city life. Today, Guido and I own over eighty homes in this village and collect a reasonable rent from each of them. We are not greedy, nor do we want to sell off anything. Our rental incomes satisfies are needs. They will continue to do so, but that is up to you."

"What do you mean by that, Uncle Joe? Maria asked. "You already know that answer," he replied and said, "but what you don't know is that I would like to see both of you live here because I would like for these nails to remain a secret. If the church or government learns of them they will find a way to take them. The church has no right to them whatsoever because when your ancestor Gordano was taking nails off the crosses the church was up in Germany burning women at the stake. In France too, if my memory serves me correct. So there you have it, a story that no one would or wants to believe and two billion dollar worth of gold that everyone would kill for. And listen, the only one who can inherit anything from me is Maria because she is an Italian citizen and signing over the deeds to our land and houses would be a simple matter. For you Robert, you would have to become an Italian citizen because you were born in the United States. You can apply, of course, but I have a feeling that with the time it takes, that Guido and I probably won't be around to see you take the oath of allegiance. You see, Guido also has a bad heart….this dear, dear friend of mine"… he said while he patted Guido's arm.

Uncle Joe poured himself another shot and continued, "The only way we can continue to keep our secret is to have it passed on to a member of our family. And the only reason I asked you to type the story is in case you don't want our homes, and in that case, we have something to give to the government to explain the gold in these holes. They won't believe the story of course, but what the hell; what else can we do."

"First of all, you old goats," Maria said in a stern voice, "is that you are not going to die. And second, is that we are going back to the United States. Do I make myself clear?" I saw Uncle Joe sadly nod his head, Guido too. "And then," she added, "After we give our landlord a few weeks' notice and apply for passports for the kids, we are coming back here to stay with you. I can home study the kids until we can arrange for a private tutor. And then…." Maria broke into tears and put her arms around Uncle Joe and Guido.

Dutchman's Gold

The roadway was clear up ahead, you could see for miles and with the sun's glare it looked as if the roads were wet. Did you know that Frank Sinatra once said, "I never met a man I didn't like"! I kind of put a twist on that with, "I've never met an ugly woman"! Think about it! I shook my head then, the mind sure does wander when you're driving cross country. My son Keith was sitting over on the passenger's seat of our old Buick. I looked over at him and said, "Hey man, what's on those pages?" I think he was trying to ignore my stupid comment, for he just sat there' or rather lying down with his feet hanging out the window. "Slurrrp!" was his response.

"What part of the English language is that?" I asked. "Sorry Dad," he said, then added, "I was in the middle of a long drink and a piece of ice got stuck in the straw." "What size is that?" looking at his unusually large plastic cup. "144 ounces Dad, replied, "It's called a Big Whop!" I couldn't believe the size of that cup and said, "Save the container, you can take a bath in it once we get up to the cabin. And by the way, what's that book you're reading, looks interesting?" It's by Jules Verne," he said. "Its' not 20,000 Leagues under the Sea, is it?" I responded. "It's called Journey to the Center of the Earth," he replied, "and I like it; I'm on Chapter 6 now."

It started to rain, a sudden summer downpour; and I slowed down to 55 mph. "Keith," I said, "roll up your window please." "Sure Dad," he responded, then added, "Are we there yet?" "Hate to tell you this son," I answered, "but we are still in Texas; and have been since yesterday." "You're kidding, right?" he asked. "There's a road sign coming up on your right," I remarked. Keith read the sign out loud: "State Line 125 miles, Prescott 368 miles, Phoenix 484 miles." I had to smile at him then, and said, "It looks like we still have a long ways to go, so six back and relax."

It wasn't long before he got restless again and was looking around the inside of the car. "What's in the metal box Dad? Is it Grandpa's?" "Answer to your first question is paper, and the answer to the second one is yes, I replied, then said "Are there any other questions?" "Yes sir," he said, "Can I look inside? I mean, if it's alright with you, I'll understand if it's personal." "What's mine is yours, you know that," I replied, then "We have a least another half hour or so before we need to gas up again, so go ahead and squeeze through to the back seat."

An hour later and a tank full of gas, we were back on the road. I told Keith that the guy at the station said he knew of a short cut over to Apache Junction. I wanted to get to the Ranger's Station before sundown. I hadn't told Keith yet the extent of his Grandpa's will. For all Keith knew is that we were getting to spend a few days at Grandpa's cabin, just outside of Apache Junction; "10 miles as the crow flies"…so said the guy back at the gas station. The entire southern section of the Superstition Mountain range is a vast area of national wilderness. However, the southern tier mountain itself; was deeded to my Dad. I'm told that it has been put off limits to everyone since my Dad died last year. I needed to contact the Park Ranger to let him know that I would be staying on the mountain for a while.

I haven't since Jimmy ever since we were teenagers. I had stayed with my Dad for a few summers back then and Jimmy and I got to be inseparable. When World War II broke out and I ended up in Africa with Patton and Jimmy became a Wind-talker on Guadalcanal. I wondered if he would remember me since I've become bald. Then I remembered too that the telephone at the ranger's station is probably still out; for Keith said he had tried over twenty times to contact the station.

"Is it a treasure map?" Keith asked. I almost choked on that suggestion. "No son," I replied, "It's just a map of the mountain showing locations of Grandpa's cabin and various watering holes." "Okay Dad," I responded, "but it sure looks old." I then added to his question and said, "I believe there are two sides of the map. One side depicts watering holes and known trails; the other side roadways and property lines." I saw him picking up a bracelet from the box. "Who's this belong too, is it Mom's?" He asked. "Mom has one just like it and this is just an extra one I guess," I answered; then added, "If you look close, you can see that the charms are actually planets: the Sun, Moon, Saturn, and the Red one I guess is Mars." "Is it gold, Dad? He asked. "I don't think so son," I said, "it looks like real gold but with a lighter yellow color, maybe it is what they call fool's gold; but I'm not really sure."

The ranger was walking out to his truck when we pulled up. Just in time, I thought. I got out of our car and said, "You don't remember me, do you?" Then it struck him…"Billy! You're the Billy who used to go climbing with me up at the Needles. Well, I'm be damned. Even with no hair, I'd still recognize you anywhere. And I'll bet that scar over your right eye came from an arrow?" "You just had to bring that up, huh!" I responded. Then I explained to Keith that Jimmy and I had played together when we were kids. Every summer my Mom would go off to Europe with her boyfriend and she would drop me off here to stay with your Grandpa. He didn't like me much, didn't even want me around; so I was left to wander around this mountain all by myself. That's how Jimmy and I met up, over at the Indian reservation at Apache Wells. Fact is, it was Jimmy's uncle who had sold the mountain to your grandpa, just so the Federal government couldn't steal it away from the Indians. Your Grandpa actually was deeded the entire mountain range, but at the urging of then President Roosevelt, he let the government have the range. All 800 square miles of it, as long as it remained a national forest and the Indians' had rights of access as long as they chose to. The only exception was Superstition Mountain, which was split in half. The northern half was to remain an Apache reservation, while the southern continued to belong to your Grandpa… tax free. It was part of the deal he made with the President. We also control mineral and well as water rights." "In short," Jimmy said, "Your Grandpa was a very, very smart man."

'Look Dad," Keith pointing over to Jimmy's arm, "he's wearing a bracelet just like yours on his right wrist." "I sure am," Jimmy relied, "Your Grandpa gave this to me, and he also gave one to my wife. In fact, he told me that he had given one to your Mom too. I guess it is the fourth one your Dad has." Then before I got a chance to say anything, he added, "You guys better come in and sit down, I have a lot to explain to you. Besides, it's dark now; you would have a hard time finding the cabin. And let me call my wife, you remember Running Water, don't you Billy?"

"Well, not really," I had to admit, then added, "I'm sorry to say; but we were really young then, and I guess I was more concerned with frogs and worms back then." We all had to laugh at that. Jimmy then called his wife and made a pot of coffee. We sat down inside his office, and looked around the walls. There were a lot of Indian mementos hanging, some looked really old. The coffee sure smelled good and just as it was ready, there was a knock on the door. Jimmy opened the door and their stood Running Water, holding two big buckets of KFC and a large bag of biscuits. We sat down and became reacquainted again. I did remember a little short dark haired girl at the reservation school we played at during the summer months. I didn't know if she was the one that I had dipped her pony tail into the white glue. She must have read my mind, and just smiled at me. "Oops," I said, she was!

"You know Billy," Jimmy began, "Your Dad was good to Running Water and I. We took care of him just before he died. The Sheriff at Apache Wells and I are still after the ones that pushed him over the cliff at Beaver Springs." "Pushed! I was told he committed suicide." I retorted. "Afraid so Billy, for my cousin Eagle Tail was there hunting for quail near the ravine; he saw the whole thing. But he wasn't close enough, because his descriptions of the two men were vague; and I'm afraid the trail is getting colder. But that's not what I was going to say." He continued. "Your Dad wanted to ensure his mountain was safe long after he was gone. He made Running Water and I swear a solemn oath that we would find you and ensure that you get settled in. He knew that you were never going to live here, but he hoped that you would come and stay a while; and perhaps eventually change your mind. It was his dream that you maintain Superstition.

I looked at Running Water and Jimmy and said, "I honestly can't answer that at this time, after all Keith and I just got here. We came up here to stay a couple of weeks, to check things out as your telegram requested. We both have responsibilities back in Austin: my job, Keith's school, and my wife…can't forget about her you know!" Running Water had to laugh at that, and said, "I'd like to meet her sometime."

Just then a coughing sound came from the rear of the office and a voice asked, "Isn't it time you introduced me?" "Oh God," Jimmy said, "Sorry sir, but it's just that I hadn't seen Billy since before the war. Everyone," Jimmy continued, "this is the President of the United States." I looked at my son, who just stood there with a chicken leg in his mouth. "Sit down folks," the

President said, "Let's not me so formal tonight. And Running Water, the guys in the back want to thank you for the fried chick and biscuits." I was wondering why she was carrying two buckets of chicken, now I know.

"Running Water, please tell him, I can't seem to find the right words." Jimmy said. Running Water looked at me and said, "You really have no idea what your Dad has done for you." She said as a matter of fact. Then she continued, "He told me himself that he couldn't regain all those years you two were apart, that he had wanted but just couldn't be there for you. Superstition Mountain was his mistress, was his life. He spent more than fifty years on the mountain before he died, and when he did die; he was a very rich man."

The President was sitting next to her and hadn't said a word. She continued, "I am sure that you have heard of the Dutchman's Gold that was discovered by the Indians here in these mountains. Your Dad was the Dutchman and probably is the reason why he was murdered." "Keith spoke up then and said, "So, where is the money?" Jimmy interjected then and said, "That part is complicated. You see," the continued, "you see Keith, your Grandpa was attempting to give the money back to its owners. He had arranged to meet with the President of the United States, but that telegram got into the wrong hands. Running Water and I believe that with your help, we can use the Apache Nation to act as liaison and to run interference with the local bad guys." 'Is there really that much gold?" Keith asked. Running Water just smiled and asked, "Do you have a swimming pool at home?" "Yes," Keith replied, "a big one with an 8 foot deep end." "Well," she responded, "close your eyes and imagine that your swimming pool is filled with gold instead of water. Do you think that is a lot of gold?" "It sure is," Keith replied. "Now," Running Water continued, "multiply that by ten and you'll see the kind of problem we have." "You got to be kidding!" I said. Jimmy then added, "And that's not even including the money that we have waiting for you at our bank, the one on our reservation; not in town."

I was just thinking for a moment, then suddenly it occurred to me. "Why did they call him the Dutchman?" I asked to no one in particular. "Our family has English roots, coming across from the Carolinas; then the Appalachians… and finally Texas. "I can answer that one," the President said. "It seems that Teddy Roosevelt came to Superstition Mountain hunting for pheasant. There were plenty of them around these parts in those days, and the Indians didn't care much for their meat. But Teddy came up with a recipe that eventually was copied the world over. But it was when he was here, having breakfast with your Dad; that he noticed he loved eating Scrapple. Now, there is two things that was known for a fact then: one was that Scrapple was made from pig's parts, and two; only Pennsylvania Dutch people ever ate it. The President called him the "Dutchman" after that and it stuck!"

"I was hoping that the map in Grandpa's box was a treasure map, and we were going to use it to go after gold!" Keith said. "Let me see that map please," Running Water said. She spread the map on the table and ran her hands over the cloth until the surface was smooth, the said, "Yes Keith, this is a treasure map of sorts. Your Grandpa told us about this map, he said that it was a direction finder; whatever that is. He also told us that our bracelets were the key to this map." "Why are there two sides?" Keith inquired. Both Running Water and Jimmy looked at the maps very carefully, constantly changing from one side to the other; attempting to compare the two. Keith was holding our bracelet and said, "These are supposed to be planets, right? And if they are, shouldn't there also be planets on the map?" "We all stared at the map for quite some time now. Jimmy made another pot of coffee and Keith was finishing off another chicken leg when he said, "Wait a minute Dad, move your hand please?" I looked down and noticed that I had my hand over one corner of the map. I removed it, and there was the Sun. "Turn the map over please," said Running Water, and then added, "And over here in this corner is the Moon. These are maps of the mountain in the day and at night. "Look," said Jimmy, "there's lines going down from the moon to the mountain, but I guess they are just the moons rays shining down on the mountain. " Keith picked up his copy of Jules Verne's book and showed Running Water the picture of the sun's rays shining through a port hole on the side of the volcano and the sun's rays pointing to the entrance into middle earth. "I count nine Moon rays," said Keith, "but only one of the rays touches down on the mountain." "There," Running Water said, "right there! I know exactly where that is. That must be the entrance to the mine your Grandpa wanted us to find."

The President made a coughing sound, then another one, and yet two more before he finally said, "Excuse me for interrupting, but I have been quiet in the back here and making sure that you folks are the real deal. I have no doubt's that Billy is Gus's son and now is the time for me to let you all in on the truth. I hope I can trust you all. "Please sir, take my seat," Jimmy said. "Thank you son," the President said, then "now let's get a few facts straight here. First of all, Gus is not the Dutchman I tried to make you believe. Sorry about that, but I wanted to test you. You all seemed to be genuinely buying that story. Fact is, I happen to like Scrapple myself, and just threw that in."

The President paused a moment, took a sip of coffee; then continued. "Gus was a very good person, a very good friend; who trusted with my life. He and I were partner's way back when he and I first came to these hills. Miners back then always partnered up, you'd go crazy talking to yourself. Eventually Gus married. His first wife was an Apache women, Little Feather was her name. The U.S. Calvary took her life in a raid on her village, it was winter; and the braves were known to be inside their teepees. They were married only a year and is one of the reasons he was deeded these mountains. President Roosevelt wanted a federal wildlife refuge in these parts and we let him have most of the upper mountain range, leaving the lower range to Gus. By that time, and with the aid of the entire Apache Nation, we collected gold from various locations and had some of the boxes transferred to by the U.S. Calvary to Fort Knox. Other boxes of gold we kept at the bank in Apache Wells."

   The President smiled then, and said, "Somewhere along the way, Gus married Maria; your grandmother Keith. She hated Apache Junction and got bored living here. She took up with a guy that was vacationing from Europe and they left, going back to Europe to never been seen again. She had no idea that Gus and I had found gold. But there was also another gold mine which I let Gus take the credit for finding. You see, I was a Prospector, but I had also been a Senator from Kentucky in the past. I wanted to return to that life, and knew if I was labeled a "Prospector," I wouldn't have a chance to run for the Presidency. Gus tried to give me more gold than I needed, but I only wanted enough to help me with the campaign and win the election. I have a wife in the White House, a mansion in New York; even Carol's family is in investments and very well off. I easily could have used her money for the campaign, but felt it would be better if I didn't. I think Gus and I made the right decision in that regard."

"Now, let's get back to the matter at hand. The gold that is hidden here in Scribes Valley is a cache that I ran across by accident. Gus and I found out later from Jimmy's grandfather that this gold was from several other gold strikes in California and from train and bank robberies. How this gold came to Superstition I'll never know, but it had. Several boxes had the names of mines, and several bags of gold still had their owner's tie cord still secured around them. I recall some of the mines names too. Let's see, there was the Lost Peg Leg Smith's mine in southern California, Sutter's Mill up near Sacramento; and the Peralta Mine north of here. Even Billy the Kid's gold his stole from the town of Tombstone is here. And even more than you can image when you consider that hundreds of bags of Mexican gold is here that the Wild Bunch brought back from across the Rio Grande."

The President paused again, then said as a matter of fact, "What is of particular interest to me, as President of these United States, is the vast amount of gold that was stolen from Fort Knox. I know that the knowledge of the robbery was kept from the public, but I was there when they stole it, and it will be returned to the American people."

"You're the Dutchman!" Keith said with a surprised look on his face. "Yes son," the President replied, "and that is why it is so important to return the gold that still is hidden away, the gold which rightfully belongs to others; even though some of it will be hard to return. I had Gus take dynamite and blow the original entrance to the cavern, and conceal a new entrance. I believe you now have found that new entrance. So, if you will permit me, I would like to accompany you on your expedition into the caverns of Superstition. I don't think we have to worry about any bad guys hanging around, but just in case, tomorrow morning I will have several units of the Army National Guard here to protect and provide security for this area. Okay with you guys?"

"Can I come too?" asked Keith. "Of course," replied the President. Then he looked at Jimmy and me and said, "I would expect that you would like to finish what you had started. And one more thing, I checked with the bank at Apache Junction. Okay, I have to admit I was just curious; but anyways you should know that Gus had deposited gold that he had himself found while prospecting alone. The gold was rightfully his, and he deposited it in Jimmy and Billy's names; both you boys were very special to him. He made the bank ensure in writing that the gold would be divided equally between you two. Well, less ten percent, that he left to Running Water for use for various charities of the Apache Nation." "That portion still needs to be co-signed by both parties," Running Water interjected, then she grinned and said, "but that leaves you two over 300 hundred million dollars to spit between yourselves." Keith said it all when he blurted out, "Cool!"

We were a party of twenty-four, heading out from the ranger station in jeeps and four-wheel drive SUV's. After about an hour we finally arrived at entrance indicated on the map. It took a while for Jimmy and several National Guardsmen to remove grass and overgrown shrubs which concealed the entrance. But it was only Jimmy, Running Water, Keith, and the President and I who were allowed to enter. Two secret service guards began complaining, saying that they had to enter to protect the President. I came to understand very quickly the greed that the Superstition creates in people, and didn't say a word when the President said "No, you and everyone else will wait here…do I make myself clear!" He wasn't smiling when he said that, and I then realized that he wasn't kidding when he said he was the Dutchmen; still protective of his beloved Superstition.

The President came prepared, with lanterns and flashlights to illuminate the way into the cavern. Gus had made it easy for our accent, by removing boulders and other debris from the main tunnel. After we walked about three hundred feet, we entered a large chamber. Jimmy and I ran lanterns along the cavern walls, placing them approximately twenty feet apart. Turing the lanterns to their highest setting, the cavern lit up like a street in Vegas. Everywhere you looked were stacks of gold: coins, bars, and chain. Hundreds of gold bricks that had the U.S. stamp on them indicated that they came from the vaults at Fort Knox. Running Water and Jimmy began taking photographs, but were asked to stop by the President. He said, "It would be too embarrassing for me and our nation if anyone found out that I had known of this all along. The political ramifications alone would certainly cause a rally for my impeachment. My intention is to have the U.S. gold moved to Fort Knox. There are several stronghold beneath the fort that can serve as storage facilities for these other caches until we can find a better place, or their rightful owners. Now to reiterate, if you please ladies and gentlemen, no one must know of this! Yes, I know what you're thinking, that just a portion of all this could wipe out our national debt. But believe me, a nation cannot survive without a national debt; many other countries have failed because they thought they could."

It took exactly two weeks for the National Guard to move the gold, eventually loading over one hundred and sixty trucks. The trip to Fort Knox took fourteen hours and they had no incidents during the entire period. Looking around the cavern, Jimmy and I were the last ones to leave; putting out the lanterns one by one. We left them there, along with several large bags of gold Pesos. The President decided to leave the Mexican gold behind, and he didn't elaborate as to why; and we didn't ask. I reached into one of the bags and took out six gold Pesos. I wanted to make key chains out of them for each of us…our little remembrance, our little secret. As we left the cave the National Guard took over and placed charges, from the entrance all the way to cavern. The resulting explosion left several tons of rock which completely changed the landscape. Then the Major of the Guard placed a sign directly in front of the landside: "Private Property --- Keep Out."

Keith and I returned to Austin. We gave the Apache Nation a one hundred year lease on our portion of the mountain and now it is patrolled by Apache reservation police. Jimmy and Running Water are doing find and are now expecting their first child. My wife, well she was upset with me for when I left I also left behind my job. You see, the supervisor had called her inform me that I no longer had a job. Nice guy, huh! Keith couldn't help laughing, he knew I was making only seven fifty an hour on a job that was getting me nowhere. Then Keith showed her the check Running Water gave us from the bank. "It's only half," I told her, and said Running Water suggested that we keep the rest in the bank for our future, and Keith's future…I couldn't agree more.

We're doing well now, paying off our house and buying a brand new Buick. I didn't go back to work, telling everyone that I was retired and spent my entire time coaching Keith's baseball and football leagues. And it was my wife who rented a limo and drove to my old job at Solano Security. She said I should have seen the look on my supervisors face when she handed him my old badge and uniform…and then watched as she got back into the limo and drove off….priceless!

The Last of the Clurichaun's

Found beneath several layers of dirt, next to an underground river; inside a large cavern at Cumea were these tablets. Written in a combination of Irish and Latin, I copied them down as best I could; for the world needs to know of this…

"If you are reading this, then you have discovered these clay tablets I have left behind. Please, don't destroyed them. You must understand that these tablets contain our history, our only written record, of an Irish clan who had been made to leave their beloved Ireland many hundreds of years ago.

After many, many years of traveling from one country to the next, and never being able to call on place home because we are different, we had finally come to Cumae. But the journey had been long and arduous, with many of us dying along the way. From famine, to the wide spread plaque which effected most of Europe, and from the lack of proper food and sunlight from living beneath the ground… all these contributed to our demise.

It was at the sulfur springs in Solfatara that we discovered an underground river that had led us here beneath this old Greek colony called Cumae. And it is thanks to the very same river that we have not been discovered... apparently until now. You must have come through the opening that led to the underground river. We had learned through the years that people believed that this river was the actual river Sphinx, and river that led to the unknown region called Hades.

It should be noted that if you travel south along the underground river you will eventually come to Sofatara, where we entered. And if you travel north, as we hope you will, then you will come to a waterfall which cascades down into our lake and the underground city.

I am writing the last tablet, but I considered it necessary to also write this; although it is becoming extremely difficult for I am dying. I fell from the mushroom cliff in the darkness and broke my leg; the bone now protruding from the skin and the blood now flowing freely. If I don't get to finish the last table, I want you to know that I am Wallgrass; and this is our story, the story of a lost clan of Irish people... the clan Clurichaun. I have numbered these....

Tablet 1

My name is Wallgrass, and I am the last of my clan. Kneeling here at the water's edge, I looked across the inland lake, a vast cavern deep in the earth's crust. Our clan had lived here now for some hundred years or so, since the time the sun people from above drove us down into the earth. Leprechaun's there were called, fierce a times, a loving tribe during better days.

I glazed downward, looking upon the body of my mother; who passed away a few hours ago. She would have been three scores times ten, as the Leprechaun's would say. The funny thing is, she outlived many of our people whom she helped bring into this world. Even her two closest friends passed away several years ago.

I placed a wreath of fern that I gathered from several braches that grew under the waterfall that fell into the lake. I looked down again at her frail body, and thought of what she requested of me just a few days ago. "Wallgrass," she would say in her whisper like voice, "Mate with me, this manner it is possible to continue our clan… we can bear both a male and female child." She understood when I refused her request, but I could see in her eyes that she was sadden because our past, our history such as it was; was coming to an end.

Her last request of me was simple… "Wallgrass," she said with a look of great concern on her face, "tell our story…" Her eyes closed after those few words, and I knew she had died. I was alone now, really alone; for I was truly the last of our clan.

Tablet II

I buried my mother among her own kind at a burial place we had chosen many years ago. Located in the center of our inland lake, a small island had formed during a violent earthquake; the land mass pushing up through the crystal clear waters of the lake. Helmush it was called, named such by our leader for the soft rocky terrain which he deemed appropriate for a burial site.

Remembering my promise, I sat down at the table my Uncle Fearghal had made. It was an overly large table, big enough to hold the flat iron discs which we used for plates. He had made a bench from wood and that had turned into stone; a present for my mother. Sitting there, I could look across the inland lake, a small lake compared to others I have seen above ground years ago. But this was our lake… and the water was pure.

It took me several days to find enough soft stone to make into a tablets for writing. I wasn't sure how many I would need, so I collected all the soft stones I could find. I molded them into square flat plates and piled them up next to the table. I also cut several lengths of tree roots which I carved into writing sticks.

I don't know how long I just sat there, but after a while I got up and washed myself in the lake. There were plenty of root vegetables available nearby and I boiled several for my dinner. And again, I just sat staring at the lake. I knew when it was daylight above ground because the water was warmer than when the sky is dark. And I knew when it was cold above because then a mist would rise from the lake. "It must be night time and very cold above," I thought out loud to myself.

I picked up a clay tablet and placed it upon the table. I let my mind wander... many evenings my mother and I would sit with the others around our fire pit. I remembered the stories I had heard, telling about the feats of our clan from the very beginning to the time the Leprechaun's drove us beneath the earth.

Suddenly it occurred to me that the best way to tell our story, our history, is to write it down just the way I remember hearing them, in their words, and in the words from those before them. This would be right.

I found a goblet that my mother had always used and lowered into the lake. She said it had once belonged to a family of Leprechaun's. The clear, cool water was refreshing. I picked up a writing stick... then again remembered my promise. If there was one thing that could be said about our clan… that would be that a Clurichaun always keeps his promise

Tablet III

From the words of Padraig, as told by Ruadhri, as told by Brion, Diarmaid:

It was during a cold winter's evening, with his wife Brid sitting by his side next to the great fire; that our great ancestor Ardghal declared that we should attempt to keep away from the larger humans. Life was good now, with plenty of meat stored in the ice cave, and grain in clay pots in which they traded for meat with Fearghus. Fearghus was the village butcher; being much larger than most; almost as tall as the watch tower.

There was much to do in our small village. The taller people did most of the fishing, and the killing of deer, rams and pigs; which were too large and cumbersome for us shorter people. But for harvesting root vegetables and berries from bushes, we were much more adapted being closer to the ground.

How we became different is still a mystery; that is, some of our clan being short in stature: smaller arms, smaller legs; although our heads appeared to be of equal size. Some say it was a curse put upon our leader

Connlaodh, for it was he who mated a woman not from our village. They said she was very short and very ugly, but that is a matter of no importance. They mated, several times in fact, to produce no less than eleven children: all short in stature, like their mother.

Time passed, and their offspring discovered other people like themselves. People from all around would begin to come together for social events. And it was during these annual winter gatherings, when clans from nearby villages came together, that young men and women came to know each other.

These gathering were always held when the first white winter ground cover began to appear on our lodges. And no matter your size, be it large or small, everyone came to be with Connlaodh. For it was his ice caves that were always filled with good meat and his clay pots full of the finest grains from which he made excellent bread and a strong drink.

As friendships developed from these yearly gatherings, so did marriages between villagers; big and small alike. Years passed, and everyone began to prosper. And it was inevitable that children began to arrive… born both large and small of body; and families grew. Eventually our village alone numbered well over two hundred.

Tablet IV

From the words of Deagian, as told by Lord Tirnach, as told by Rkuadhan:

It was on a cold, misty morning; fog covering much of the green pasture in the glen that we now called home that I remember waking with a pain in my head. I was lying on the ground next to my dog. I shook my head, trying to regain my senses as I looked across the glen at our village. There were several homes built in the hollow of tree trucks. Hollus was our carpenter, and he was good with tools. In every lodge he made large holes he called windows for allowing air inside and a small doorway to enter and exit from…always facing north. Once inside you could see just how cleaver Hollus was: he fashioned a small bed for sleeping, a table for eating our meals, and a small area near the hearth for cooking. Water was brought in via a system of aqueducts which fed from a nearby stream. Somehow he managed to build levies which brought water into each home and then continued its downward path to a central fountain.

We had been living above ground now for the last hundred or so years. Our previous village near a lake above ground was invaded by larger humans, then the harsh winter with violent storms forced us to travel south to a warmer climate. Yet we still maintained an underground cavern, now used for meetings and social gatherings. We actually had several over the years, but continually changed location due to above ground drainage which flooded the caverns floor.

Our latest cavern, we now called Piarae, also was used to store nuts, potatoes, and grains. Meade, a strong drink made from fermented honey, was the invention of Hamus, who also made bread for the entire clan. No one knows where he got the knowledge, we just know that it was good. Too good, at times, for many of our men folks had drunk to excess; became foolish or fell to the ground sound asleep. I am happy to say I was one of them. Some say that was how we got the name: Clurichan.

It was on Fairies Eve, that we got word of an invading clan coming into our glen from the east. Eibhear, our best man, said that they were carrying pick axes, swords, and wearing the colors of Leprechauns. We had heard of these people and knew that they were much like us. But with them being so far south, it never entered our thoughts that they might attack us.

A Leprechaun knight, in full battle armor, rode toward us on a large black dog with news from King Conall. The king had halted his army of 700 at the southern region of our territory and sent a message of warning. It was simple and to the point: Leave Ireland, take only your women and children; and what you can carry. Leave now!

Hamus, Tadhg, and Breanan; the eldest of our clan, led us back underground.

Tablet V

From the words of Somhairie, as told by Aodan, as told by Ailli:

The year was 1366, and the news from a nearby village told us that Henry of Trastamara was ruling Spain. But that was of no importance to us, for we had gotten used to remaining beneath the surface. Ireland, for sure, despised our clan.

After a difficult journey taking two hundred years, we found a new home in what we were told was France. We numbered only seventy now, owing to deaths from several unknown diseases. We managed to survive on roots, mushrooms and fruits taken from trees above ground. Meats like mutton, chicken and horse; we exchanged with French families we had gotten to know. There were times we just took what we could find, those being desperate times.

It was strange, but these small French people, the size of our own, were much like ourselves. There were four clans in total, living in the greenwood; a forest several kilometers in circumference and a short distance from our cavern. In the center was a large fresh water lake and each clan had built a village which bordered north, south, east and west. They all shared the lake in a manner which their communities prospered. One clan tended vegetable crops in a section of the forest which they had cleared for that purpose. Another clan walked for several kilometers to orchards of apples, figs, and oranges in which they worked; and in payment, received a portion of each harvest which they stored in caves for use during the winter months. Yet another clan proved best at carpentry and from trees that had fallen from age, built homes and vessels for use upon the lake. It was Caoimhim, from the Youke clan, who we got to know very well. A gentle and friendly leader of his clan, he taught his villagers the art of fishing with poles as well as nets made from fibers spun from corn husks.

It was every quarter of the moon, or the seventh day after the last gathering, that the clans brought their goods to Caoimhim's village. There they traded equally and honestly, with no one person taking advantage of the other; for they learned from the town's local people how dishonest people never gain… always lose.

Life went on through the years and the French and Irish Clurichaun clans lived peacefully, side by side.

Eventually our clans intermingled, and life underground ceased. Those vast caverns were now used for storage of grains and fruits. That is, until the French police arrived…

Tablet VI

From the words of Eimhin, as told by Eithne, as told by Eanna:

It was in a place the French called Bordeaux, along the Vienne River, that we discovered a vast underground cavern with many anti-chambers, water falls, and streams for drinking fresh water and washing our clothes. It was the bluish, crystal clear waters of the inland lake made our decision to stay here easier.

The French police had driven us back underground, and this time we brought several families with us. It was difficult to ascertain what prompted them to confront us. We had done nothing wrong, stayed to ourselves, and paid for everything we purchased from village stores. They told us we had broken laws of which were unknown to us. They said we paid no taxes but wouldn't explain what the taxes were for. Our women were treated unfairly, pushed to the back of lines, not being able to ride on trolleys. And the general unfair treatment towards us "small" people became too much to bear. And then there was the spread of smallpox.

Tablet VII

This is the last tablet and it is being written by me, the last of our clan.

It wasn't just the sickness that had spread throughout France that decimated our clan. It was the earthquake which collapsed the western side of our cavern that led to the final blow. Entire lodges were crushed under tons of rock, killing our remaining nine families.

Mother and I rebuilt our lodge, but just to keep ourselves occupied. We had nowhere to go, and mother was too weak to travel even if she wanted to.

I brought out the last flask of Meade from the storeroom. I poured out the water from my goblet and filled it to the brim with Hamus's fine liquor. I remembered the good days with Hamus, his telling old stories, and both of us getting so drunk that we slept next to the barrels of Meade.

The sickness that took my mother was apparently effecting me. More Meade wouldn't cure me, but it sure

will past the time. Somehow I can now remember
Hamus's recipe for his special brew, and easy one too,
with the addition of cinnamon we had harvested.

   The recipe is…"

Giuseppe

It was six o'clock in the morning when the train pulled into the Piazza Garibaldi station. I was looking out the glass windows at the passenger train opposite our track; sleek and brand new. It also had just pulled into the station, with its wheels screeching to a halt, with smoke pillowing from underneath the powerful engines.

I grabbed my still wet backpack and departed the train. It had been raining when we left Milano at midnight, but you could tell that the rains haven't come this far south because the station's platform was dry.

I took out my map of downtown Naples, and checked the direction I needed to walk to get to my Grandmother's old house. I was sort of on a quest, fulfilling a promise I had made; that I would write the story she had told me before she died. I also promised her that I would come to Italy to see her home, and especially the little courtyard that her home was situated in. Only then, she would say, can you convey the meaning of my story.

I left the train station and couldn't help but notice the huge statue of Giuseppe Garibaldi off to the left. I found Via Carbonara, when after two blocks turned into Via Maria Longo. I was looking for Piazza Cavour when I suddenly realized I was standing right dab in the middle of the main square. The square was huge and already filled with shoppers on this early Saturday morning. I rechecked my map and crossed to the opposite side of the square. I found the street I was looking for, Via San Giuseppe del Nudi. It was a very narrow and I had to keep stepping into the entry ways of stores to keep out of the way of traffic. Finally, I saw the tiny sign that I was looking for, "Abruzi". My grandmother mentioned that there would be a small archway that led to a courtyard.

I entered the courtyard, which by comparison; would be the size of a double car garage in America. To the right was the small stop that once belonged to Giuseppe, and just to the right of the shop was a small doorway that led upstairs to my Grandmother's house. I turned around and looked around the courtyard. Next to Giuseppe's shop was a small bake shop, then two apartments; for there were two doors: one for downstairs, and one leading upstairs. Finally, just before exiting under the archway out onto the street was a tiny flower shop; where several large vases of rose's being displayed.

I was startled when someone approached me from behind and asked me in broken English if she could help me. Then, and I guess it was because of my Italian complexion, she said, "Your Johnny, I know you from your photograph; your Maria's grandson from America."

We sat down at a small table in front of Giuseppe's shop. My grandmother had apparently kept her very well informed because she knew everything about me. She knew when I graduated from high school, knew that I joined the Marines and had to go to Vietnam; even my getting married a couple of years ago. And then she said something that really surprised me. She said that she knew why I had come to Italy. Then she added, "And I know that you already know a lot about Giuseppe, but I think I know maybe a little bit more. But for now, young man, let me get you some sweet pasta and coffee. And by the way, my name is Giovanna. A few minutes later, as she poured the expresso; she began.

"The story about Giuseppe really starts just before the war broke out between France and Germany. He and his mother had been living in Milano before he was drafted. A year later, Giuseppe was a promoted Sergeant in the Italian Army; assigned to border patrol near the Swiss Alps. Just before the war ended, he was walking with his squad along a mountain pass when one of his men stepped on a land mine that was near them. After the explosion, Giuseppe could hardly hear and his speech was slurred. He was only twenty-two years old and had to leave the Army that he had grown to love. He couldn't hold a job, so he came with his mother to Naples; to be near old friends of hers. It was a short man, a cobbler by trade; named Luigi who had this small shop you're sitting on front of. He took Giuseppe on as his apprentice. Luigi also made small wooded figurines using a small saw and soon Giuseppe began doing the same."

Giovanna stopped for a moment, finished her coffee, and continued, "Luigi died about two years later and left the shop to Giuseppe. Everybody was buying shoes in Pizza Garibaldi, and soon Giuseppe limited his trade to shoe repair. But the figurines became his passion. H would go into the country to find wood. He would never steal though, always asking if he could have some broken limbs off apple, cherry, walnut, or oak trees. I have a figurine in my home that Giuseppe made for my mother. It is made from hazelnut. His own mother eventually died and he was left alone with the shop."

She paused, looked at me, and said, "Your grandmother move into the apartment upstairs, and Giuseppe worked and lived in his own little shop. He became a quiet man, keeping to himself. Everyone knew he was poor, and everyone thought it was a shame the way our government treated him, not giving him some sort of disability after he was discharged. And every morning, right at five o'clock; Giuseppe would come out onto our courtyard and sweeps the cobblestones. He never asked for money, he just felt it was his job. And he had friends, although he couldn't remember names very well; so for every day of the week when they came by he would give that day's name:

Lunedi (Monday), would be Senior Lunedi, the bread man. His shop was right next to Giuseppe's and everyday he would always give Giuseppe two loaves of bread: one loaf would be fresh and the other would be a day old. The old bread would be for soup, Senior Lunedi would tell him

Martedi (Tuesday) would be for Senora Martedi, the vegetable lady. She always placed in a paper bag an onion, two stalks of celery, and two carrots; the laid the bag on top of this small table…right in front of his shop. She would add some oregano sprigs or basil leaves when she had extra. "For the soup," she would always say.

Mercoledi (Wednesday) would be the newspaper man from around the corner. He always came into Giuseppe's shop on rainy days. They would put up and awning over his small table, then get two chairs; and

drink wine. But it was on Wednesday's that Senor
Mercoledi would bring a small piece of cheese, a loaf of
garlic bread and a piece of dry salami. Giuseppe would
always bring out a carafe wine, red or white, or sweet or
dry…it didn't matter. Old Luigi had kept wine in a
small cellar under his shop and over the years had
collected many, many bottles.

Giovedi (Thursday) would be Mrs. Giovedi with
her cart full of kitchen items, laundry soaps, mops,
brooms, and sometimes fruit. The women who lived in
the courtyard would all come out of their apartments
when she arrived to buy her goods. Sometimes a senora
living upstairs would come out onto her balcony and call
down for what she needed. Mrs. Giovedi would tell her
the price, then the senora would place the money in a
small basket tied to a rope. She would lower the basket
with the money inside. Mrs. Giovedi would take out the
money and put the item or items the senora purchased
inside…and the basket would be raised. The other
vendors would also use this method from time to time,
especially when it was raining. Giuseppe would barter
sometimes with Mrs. Giovedi, trading something he had
made for what he needed.

Venerdi (Friday) was my own mother who ran
the fish shop back then. You can still see those fish tubs
over there that I now use for flowers. Senora Venerdi,

he would call her, and always used the proper address; calling her "Senora" even though they lived next to each other. And every Friday, come rain or shine, my mother always put one large fish inside wrapping paper and then placed the fish on top of this table. If she had extra lemons, she would always give him one or two. And during the holidays, she would always put a great big bag of mussels along with the fish on the table. He tried to pay her once, but she insisted that the fish didn't come from her shop.

Sabato (Saturday) was Senor Sabato who lived upstairs over the fish shop. She worked as a seamstress over on Via Droumo, a local sweat shop. Even though she worked for pennies, she would always find the time and extra cloth from the trash bins to make shirts and pants; even dresses for the people in our courtyard. One Christmas she gave Giuseppe a red shirt and I think he wore that shirt until I turned pink from so many washings.

Domenica (Sunday) was our priest from across the street at the cathedral. He was in the Army with Giuseppe and befriended him. Those were terrible times and sometimes when the snows arrived and they were huddled inside caves, Giuseppe would carve figurines for the Presepe (or Nativity scenes) for the father's cathedral here in Naples. Father Domenica gladly accepted them, saying he would save them for Giuseppe. Now they are in the cathedral among others that Giuseppe had made. The Presepe contains a huge miniature display of several villages where men and women are seen drinking and eating at local inns, working in the fields, fishing along streams, or an old man lying on his front door step, drunk from drinking too much wine. And if you were to look closer at the markets, you could see dozens of miniature baskets full of fish, vegetables, even bottles of wine, all with exquisite detail. The homes, the people, the animals…such detail."

"Now, Mr. Johnny," Giovanna said, "let me tell you something that I know you were never told. Look across the way there, the apartment with the green door, used to live a small girl with her mother. The father was killed in the war and the mother did odd jobs and helped her daughter as much as she could. Maria was crippled, with one leg being shorter than the other. Even though I did not keep an eye on Giuseppe all the time, I know it was him who kept hanging gifts of food and such for the family."

"On Mondays, he would take the fresh loaf of bread and place it on their doorstep. On Tuesday's, I would see him take two bottles of wine and place them next to their mailbox. Wednesday's, he would always take the cheese that he told Senora Mercoledi he was saving later over to them. Thursdays, he would take the big box of soap that I saw him buy and wait until dark. Then just before he started to sweep the courtyard, he would place it next to her door. And on Friday, he would take the fish that my mother gave him; and clean and remove the head and tail. Then he would rewrap the fish in clean paper and take it over to them. The head and tail he would use for soup, using the onion, celery, and carrots given to him by Senora Martedi. If there were fresh herbs, he would throw that in too. And every now and then I would see him put two small jars of salt and pepper and place them inside the wrapper with the fish. And on Saturday, I would see him take a small collection envelope he had borrowed from the church, and put a few coins inside, and place the envelope inside Senora Sabato's mailbox. Then one Sunday morning, when I saw him from my window; I started to cry. He would be sitting down at this very table at five o'clock in the morning reading the bible by lamplight which hung over our courtyard. He had no electricity in his shop.

I was just a small girl then, but I remember coming to his shop. He never spoke much, I thought it was because he was too embarrassed from the sound of his own voice, but I knew he was glad to have my mother and me for company. Your grandmother told me how he made some of the tools he used. For a sander to smooth his wood, for example, he would sometimes go down to the junk yard and find old kitchen strainers that were broken. He would remove the wire mess and wrap he mess very tightly around a small block of wood. He made several sanders, and he explained to me the difference. For light sanding, he would wrap the wire mess around the block of wood only once. For medium sanding, he would double wrap the wire mess. And for problem wood, he would use four or five wire mess wraps, and scrape the wood very hard.

He had only one saw, and the blade he used was of thin wire with several teeth notched into the flat part of the blade. Then he would attach the blade between a U-shape wooded handle which had been heat treated by clamping the blade at each end. He was later given a new hand saw that was made of tubular steel and had attachments to secure the blade at both ends. Still, sawing was slow…and very tedious."

"You think I could go inside the shop?" I asked. "Yes," Giovanna replied, the added, "I have the key right here." Once we entered it was like going back into history. Some of old Luigi's tools and spare parts were still lying on the benches. Giuseppe's sanders were there as well as his saws, both old and new. I picked up a saw blade and just gave it a light squeeze and it snapped into. I know that saw blades are very expensive and to use these hands tools you must have a very light touch when sawing.

I looked at Giovanna and said, "My grandmother wrote to me and said that what was inside the basement in this shop is her gift to me. That she asked Giuseppe to be the caretaker, but she kept referring to bottles and I have a hunch that what is down there is bottles of wine." Senor Giovanna just laughed then and said, "I know what is there, and yes…you should have it." We opened the trap door leading down to the basement and I took a flashlight out of my backpack. I turned the light on just as I stepped down on the damp flooring. Along the walls, in wooded crates; were stacked bottles of wine. In one corner was what my grandmother told be about. I picked up a bottle and carried it back upstairs and out to the table in the courtyard. Then I handed it to the senora who used a damp cloth to clean the exterior of the bottle. I took a bottle opener and pulled out the cork. Then Giovanna asked to smell the cork. "Beautiful," was her only word.

"Now," she said, "let me finish this story, for I have to get back to watering my plants and you have a train to catch; if I am not mistaken. Also, don't let me forget to give you a box to take six bottles back with you. You can decide what to do with the rest later, if that is alright with you?" I nodded my head, and she continued, "It was a few years, but I still remember. It was around four o'clock on a cool morning. I had gotten to close the window and heard fog horns from the direction of the Bay of Naples when I arrived at the window. I looked out, but could hardly see through the fog, but then below the old lamplight I saw little Maria and Giuseppe holding hands. They looked up at me and I could see that they were both smiling. Then there was a bright light and they were gone. No, I am not crazy, it is the truth. You see, Maria had died two weeks earlier, and everyone attended her Mass; expect for Giuseppe for he was ill. I took over chicken soup when I could, and I know the other ladies in our courtyard did the same. The Senora Sabato's minestrone was the envy of our parish. The day before I saw him with Maria, he had died."

'He left a will of sorts with Father Domenica. It's funny, you know, for I don't know the father's real name. Anyway, the good father said he left everything to you. His last wish was that you allow the church to have his miniature figures. The wine, especially the bottles that are old, ae to be enjoyed by you and your family. But if you should decide to sell them, Father Domenica says that those wrapped in red cloth should sell for about a thousand Euro's each."

I thought for a moment, then started to stammer when I said, "There are over a hundred bottles with that musty red colored strip of cloth around them…I'm rich?" "You're richer than you think Johnny," Giovanna said, then continued, "Those bottles with the red strip of cloth are from northern Italy. Father Domenica and Giuseppe drove up to Milan and brought them here after the end of the war. The bottles in wooden crates have dates on the sides of them, with the oldest dating back to 1374. After Giuseppe died, Father Domenica and I went down into his cellar. Giuseppe had quite a few statues that he wanted the father to take to his church. That was when we got a good look at those boxes. He had quite a few bottles of local wine lined up against the wall, some were red but I believe most of them are white. We both gasped when we saw several other boxes in the corner. They were not boxes of wine. What we were looking at were bottles of centuries old balsamic vinegar. Some had dates from the Spanish Inquisition, and several larger ones had King Arthur's personal crest on the sides. I counted twenty that had Napoleon's family crest engraved in what I believe is pure silver. I gave Father Domenica one bottle of the red colored balsamic for his rectory, a gesture that I knew Giuseppe would approve of. Later the good Father told me, that over the course of dinner with the Cardinal; one the server's brought the bottle and placed it on the table near the Cardinal. The Cardinal picked it up and said, "You know Father, the Bishop was telling me the other day that a bottle of balsamic from the Spanish Inquisition sold for over 8 million Euro at Sotheby's in London."

Then Giovanna said, "Young man, you are very rich!"

Cinnamon & Spice

Our three day stay at the Hotel Victoria on Capri was highlighted by several trips down into the famous Blue Grotto. Guido, our guide and boatman; told us the history of the grotto…beginning as far back at 1826. He said that the Romans, dating back to the time of Tiberius, has used this cave and placed many Roman sculptures inside. But it wasn't until the early 1800's the people began visiting regularly, and soon the grotto became the emblem of the island. And I promised Cinnamon while we were on our third trip inside that I would take her to see other grottos. I wanted her to get accustomed to being inside grottos, and caves in particular. Thus, the beginning of our story begins here, and a story that would take us literally around the world.

Several weeks later, as our plane landed at Hilo Airport, all I could think of was the Kazumura Cavern on the big island of Hawaii. Reading a bit on the history of the cavern, I discovered that it was discovered in 1836 and consists of two layers: the Upper Gallery and the Lower Gallery. I wanted to see the "castle formation" they mentioned that was located inside the Upper Gallery. I took three entire rolls of film, and it was worth the trip. The rest of the week we spent on the beach at Waikiki. Then instead of returning to the States, I changed airlines and we took off to Mexico. The travel agent at the airport was extremely helpful, and soon we were on our way to the Dos Ojos Caves; located in Cenotes Park. We stayed at the local hotel, but after seeing the caves on our first day; we checked out and rented a car so we could return in the states. I could tell that Cinnamon wasn't really impressed with what she saw.

Crisscrossing back into the United States, I decided to see the Carlsbad Caverns in New Mexico. Instead of taking the standard tour, I talked Mr. Santos, the Park Ranger; to take us on a personal tour…one that visitors normally do not get to see. We had our gear with we us and showed him our caving certificates and log book, denoting the locations and hours where we had spent beneath the surface. He wasn't too impressed, but a couple of phone calls; and we were in. "Hopefully not over our heads," said Mr. Santos who was sort of volunteered to accompanied us.

Two weeks later, we surfaced on the south side of the caverns underground system. We got lucky and assisted him in mapping a new gallery that we had found by chance on our fourth day. By then he realized that we were highly skilled caver's, way beyond the expert level. And he was so impressed with Cinnamon and the named the newly found gallery after her. Before we left, he asked for my telephone number; saving he was going back inside in the spring. It would be after the rains, and he would be honored if we would be part of his team. I wrote the dates and his phone number in my log book, this was a trip I didn't want to miss. The limestone formations here are really fantastic and they are many, many more that no one has ever seen yet.

We had already turned back in our rental car, and asked Mr. Santos to take us to the airport. We were heading back home to Florida when his assistant came up to us, saying he had an important message for us. It seems that our services were needed down under: The Jenoian Caves. Then the assistant said that he was to tell me that this was urgent.

We needed to update and refit our gear, which Mr. Santo only knew too well being a caver himself; inviting us to his home for a couple of days. He said there was a sporting goods and an Army and Navy surplus store nearby; along with the best cook in New Mexico…his wife. We must have really impressed him, for after a few phone calls; we pulled in front of the sporting goods store… at midnight! After two hours, we had our gear repacked, and were given two brand new backpacks. We had breakfast which his wife prepared for us at 4:00 in the morning…then it was off to the airport. "They need you now," he said during breakfast. Then he smiled and said, "I called your people, and they had the flight to Sidney delayed. "What do I owe you," I asked, for so far I hadn't paid for anything. He didn't respond, but as we were boarding the airline, I asked him again when I owed him. "Your people told me what you two do for a living… and you sir, don't owe anyone a thing. God bless and have a good flight." Then he helped the stewardess close the outer door.

After departing Sidney, our two hour ride by helicopter through the Blue Mountains of New South Wales was relaxing. But we didn't come to sightsee, I checked and rechecked our gear; we were needed now at Spider Cave. The other only other rescue team was deep in the Sarawak system of Malaysia and would take four days to resurface. Cinnamon and I were only a day's travel away, but I wondered just how they knew we were at Carlsbad. This was our first trip to Jenoian; and I was amazed how large the cave system was with over twenty known caves; and many subterranean caverns yet unexplored. According to their map, it appeared that Spider Cave could be reached by helicopter.

We were nearing the caves and I was listening to the pilot as he explained the situation: two girls were trapped inside the cave since yesterday. I looked down into what appeared to be huge hole in the ground with no bottom. He handed me that radio and I tried to make contact. Eventually someone radioed back, "This is Jessica, Elaine and I are trapped inside a cave; please help us." I called Jessica back on and eventually found out that they had slipped further down inside the cave, landing in a shallow pond. Elaine had sprained her wrist and Jessica said she had several deep cuts on her legs and her ankles were swollen.

The map indicated that Spider was a sheer 375 foot drop down onto the cavern floor. Jessica explained that we could not repel down due to the massive amount of vegetation along the walls and the thousands of spiders. And because of the spiders, they had to stay in the center of the shallow pond; we had to go. Manny, our crewman onboard the helicopter; wanted to hover above us with a basket. "Later," was all I said! I then strapped on a mini-parachute used for free falling, then went behind Cinnamon and ensured hers was on tight. Cinnamon saw the optimum free fall position of the helicopter and jumped out. I looked over at Manny, he looked surprised. Then I jumped right after her.

It didn't take all that long to get the girls up to another helicopter, for Manny and his team were running low on fuel and had to return. First Jessica and then Elaine went up, Cinnamon was next. After taking several photographs, I went up in the basket too. Then the girls asked to be taken back to their cabin where they were staying. It turned out to be just over the ridge, and once inside; the girls introduced us to their Mom…a registered nurse as well as a certified caver herself. Their Mom patched up Jessica, and then scolded the girls for not climbing out themselves; they've been in worse situations before. "But Mom," Elaine complained, "Those spiders were huge." We all had to laugh at that, it wasn't here comment; the expression on her face was priceless! Then the girls asked if we wanted to stay with them for the rest of the week. There was plenty of room and they didn't want to go back to Sidney…too boring they said. I could tell Cinnamon wanted to stay, and to tell you the truth; I could use the rest.

Over dinner, which turned out to be an English kidney pie; the conversation had gotten around to caving. It turned out that both girls were certified cavers, but had dropped their gear before landing in the water; which was why we didn't notice there packs in the water. I asked them if they wanted to go back into Spider, but they shook their heads and said no; those spiders could keep their packs. And besides, they were their light rigs they used for one day outings. They still had their caving rigs and heavy backpacks. I walked outside after dinner, the evening was beautiful; I could stay here a while, the view of the Blue Mountains was breathtaking.

Two days later, both girls and their Mom was ready to go again; and asked us if we wanted to join up. I had heard about the Grand Arch and the Devils' Coach House, but never of the Orient or Ribbon Caves. All three women proved to be experienced cavers, which was a relief for not having to go slow and assist those with less experience. Then Elaine suddenly had a brain spurt and said, "Wait a second, I read about you two in Caver's Magazine." It seems that Cinnamon and I were well known as being one of two rescue teams for deep cave systems. "Now," Jessica said, "I know why you guys just flew out of the helicopter, free falling over three hundred and fifty feet." "Well," I said, "We both love free falling and do it every chance we get; it's the quickest way to the bottom." "And if what your pop-up doesn't open?" Elaine asked. "That's funny," I replied, "because one time my chute didn't open and I was lucky because I landed in a lake with twenty feet of water to break my fall. And, I might add, that was the day Cinnamon and I started charging more and started using better equipment."

I didn't tell the girls, but the standard rescue gear we were issued for that particular rescue was at Clark AFB in the Philippines and was substandard. That was one of the reasons Cinnamon and I started Caver's International, a special order supply magazine. We offer through our franchise outlets only the best personal equipment and caving rigging available.

The time had come for us to leave Australia and Cinnamon and I were sitting outside their cabin. We were waiting for our transport to arrive when Elaine, Jessica and their Mom approached us. Their Mom had a couple of copies of Caver's International and showed them to the girls. When they found out that the president of the company was me, they both got excited and couldn't stop asking me how they could get a franchise here in Australia. I waited for them to calm down a bit, then looked at their Mom…the girls were serious! I called the airlines and cancelled our flight back to the States. The girls then rushed us out to their van, "were burning daylight…" the said in unison. We arrived in Sidney and talked with their lawyer who contacted mine if Florida. Hawk Henson starting to complain about it being three o'clock in the morning, but when he found out it was Cinnamon and me…he accepted the call…collect. Paper were drawn and now Jessica and Elaine have the first Australian franchise for Caver's International. I didn't know what to say when they told me that their Caver's Club of Canberra had over 2,000 members.

We finally got back to Florida and after two weeks, Cinnamon and I were sitting in 2D and 2E, seats that were only given to airline pilots or on-call aircrew personnel. I looked out the window at the small city of Auckland, located on New Zealand's North Island. I was anxious to get a look at the Waitormo Glow Worm

Caves, an expedition that we had been waiting on for some time. Once on the ground, it only took three hours by jeep to get to the caves. Cinnamon and I had our complete caving packs, for we were told that after descending into the cave we had a wet raft ride ahead of us. What the brochures tell you of this cave is right on. The black water rapids was an experience I'll never forget. And the glow worms that cling the cavern ceilings and walls…well, those you just have to see to believe.

We were in no hurry, and since we had permission to explore the western section of the caverns system, Cinnamon and I did just that. We surfaced three weeks later in a deep lagoon, covered with green ferns and moss. I took enough photos, for sure; using all twelve rolls I had with me. We also mapped out what I believe is a new section for I didn't see any marks or directional indicators that normally would be provided along the route. I will send a set of the photographs to the Caver's Society of New Zealand, along with a good map of our descent on chart paper. In one of the smaller gallery's I found a limestone formation that looked like a cocker spaniel and had sort of a light brown coloring. I didn't indicate a name to be given, leaving that to the New Zealand cavers when they go down into the gallery.

We stayed in Auckland a week, just lying around, and enjoying the local Kiwi fruit liquor. We needed a rest, and I wanted to sight see around town a bit. And besides, our next planned cave was in Lebanon, and we were waiting for our clearances to arrive. It was into the third week of our stay at the hotel in Auckland when our clearances finally came. And a whopping $2,500.00 Euro per person caving permit was attached to the already overpriced airline ticket and hotel accommodations. Well, this trip should be interesting. I have heard of the Jeita Grotto from other cavers and am told that this is one of the best. I always wanted to take a boat ride beneath the desert and was looking forward to our arrival.

We landed a little past midnight on a Monday morning in Beirut. After checking into or hotel, and getting our driver out of bed, we made plans to set out at six o'clock in the morning. Our destination was the Valley of the Dog River, or Keserwan to locals. I was hoping to see a small outpost, but instead found tourist attractions: an old fashioned train, a petting zoo, and several small gift shops and snack bars. By nine o'clock we were in our four person canoes, traveling beneath the limestone formations. Our driver was also our guide and I found out that these waters led to and from the Jeita Grotto, and made up most of what there is to see. There was one small gallery at the end of the cavern, and he took use inside. He was right, it was only used to keep spare canoes. But the entire excursion took over three hours, each way; and was one of the most relaxing experiences we had ever had. The vaulted ceilings and rocky limestone formations were breathtaking, and I didn't miss a chance to use up all the film I had brought with me.

I was thinking of heading home, when I received a telegram from Malaysia, informing us that our visa and caving clearances had been authorized. This was one cave that I definitely wanted to go into and it had always been out of bounds for U.S. citizens. I could only guess that word of my recent explorations with Cinnamon had gotten around. These were to be photographic explorations only and I had no inclination towards finding new passages. Well, at least unless they presented themselves. And when they did, at two miles beneath the surface; who was going to know. At any rate, I was really excited at hearing about Sarawak Chambers on the island of Borneo. The cavern boasts to being the largest underground pocket of air. I remembered Carlsbad, and the cavern there named Big Room…it was huge. This one I can't wait to see.

I arranged for tickets through our hotel clerk, and I had to admit; she did a wonderful job in a very short time. The only tickets available were in the first class section of the plane, but I was Borneo bound; and was glad to pay the extra. The flight turned out to be a long fourteen hours, but seems shorter for some reason. Then we hoped a helicopter for a short one hour ride, arriving at Gunung Mulu National Park. The next morning, we descended. As advertised, the cavern was in fact large enough to maneuver a helicopter inside with no problems. Our guide said that they had actually measured the space, and concluded that ten jumbo jets could easily fit…with room to spare. I was impressed, and used ten rolls of film I had packed; the cavern had numerous limestone formations and cathedral vaulted ceilings that were really intriguing. Nothing else seemed to interest us, so we decided to check into a nearby hotel. The hotel got a bit upset when Cinnamon decided to use the hot tub, but a hundred dollar bill calmed the manager down. He even brought us out a bottle of cheap champagne.

While in the process checking out, we receive another call. An emergency call from Mexico. Four cavers were trapped in the Crystal Cave of Giants, several crystal formations had shifted due to an underground earthquake. And since Cinnamon and I were the only ones available, we got the call. I was looking at Cinnamon, then I figured it out. The President of the United States had presented Cinnamon with a Medal of Freedom which she wore around her neck. Attached to the back was a state-of-the-air GPS transmitter.

I called our home office in Florida to have them fly special protective suits down to Mexico. Then I had second thoughts and called again. Cindy, one of our new sales girls was shocked when I told her to buy a first class ticket on the next available flight and get me those suits down there by tomorrow morning. And if she had too, hire a private jet. And I have to admit that I was glad I hired her, because the following morning when I got off the plane; she was standing there on the tarmac next to a helicopter.

"The suits are onboard sir," is all she said. I smiled at her and said, "Let me know when you want to go caving with Cinnamon and me?" "How about now," she replied. I just smiled and her and said, "Get in, let's go now, we are needed!" I had heard about crystal caves and I definitely wanted someone on the surface who I could trust. Without protective gear you wouldn't last fifteen minutes down there.

"We arrived at the Naica Mines and had our gear on in a matter of minutes. They had cameras situated near the entrance, and we could see that the mines were trapped by two huge twelve foot crystals which had fallen sideways. It appeared they were behind a four by four foot enclosure. "How deep?" I asked the rescue supervisor. "About four hundred, maybe less," was his response. I saw the mines manager standing by, and luckily he spoke some English. I wanted the elevator taken out of the shaft, Cinnamon and I would rappel the entire distance. I had sufficient rope with me and once we have our protective gear on I made sure my communications with Cindy was working. It was, and Cinnamon jumped into shaft with my right behind her. Next to free falling, Cinnamon loved o rappel as much as I did. We used a double rope technique I developed. It allowed both of us to rappel simultaneously with my braking by using an extra tie rope. It allowed Cinnamon the freedom to use her arms and legs to keep away from the walls.

About fifteen minutes later we found the miners, with Cinnamon squeezing her body around the crystals with ease, and together they double wrapped the rope around one of the crystals. There was already a portable winch on the opposite side of the cave and I gave it a pull. It started easily, and I gave myself a reminder to place an extra $20 in the collection box at St. Basils. Tugging on the crystals just enough for the miners to squeeze through, we had them all out from behind their would-be tomb. "Think it will hold," I asked one of the miners, "If we reinstall the elevator. I didn't see any cracks on the down." "It should," he responded, then added, "We get quakes here all the time. Only this time, we had a crystal shift, which never happened before." I radioed Cindy to ask the manager to reinstall the elevator inside the shaft and send it down. The elevator held six men, and minutes later we all were on the surface. Cindy was standing there and smiled at us. "We were lucky," I said, "It could have been much worse."

Our next destination was Miami, Florida and Cindy agreed to accompany us back. She was surprised that I had purchased three first class tickets. I just smiled and didn't say a word, she didn't need to know that our customers in Mexico were paying the bill. After we landed in Miami, I put Cindy in a cab back to our office. From there she said she could pick up her car and drive home. I also gave her the rest of the week off, and to tell the office crew that Cinnamon and I would be back in a week or so. We still had a two hour drive up the coast to our home in St. Augustine. And I knew that Cinnamon wanted to spend some time at home, maybe go on a run up and down the beach.

We took the shuttle to the Miami Airport Overnight Parking lot. At the lot's small office, attendant gave me a bill for $600.00. I paid the girl, and she just smiled. Then I have her a hundred dollar bill as a tip because I always park my Jaguar right next to her booth. "Thank You, Mr. Spice," she said, then asked, "What's your dog's name?" as she bent down to pet my collie. "Her name's Cinnamon," I replied, then added, "And she's the only certified deep cave rescue dog in the world!"

Timberline

We crashed through the pines, the snowy bank giving way to our weight; my sister first and I right behind her. We finally stopped rolling, landing on a snowy embankment, and I guessed we both passed out. I don't know how long we had been there, but apparently came to the same time when Jenny had awaken. I could see large boulders protruding though the snow here and there in the twilight. I tried to make Jenny as comfortable as possible, making a hollow in the ground between two boulders which shielded us from the bitter wind and cold. We were both hungry, and I only had a pocket knife and a few matches left. Hopefully, we told each other; we could find our way off this mountain. I guess it had been a full day now since our Pa pushed us out onto the snow.

We had been flying in his single engine Lockheed Vega aircraft when he told us our navigation and altimeter gauges were frozen. He was trying to find a place to put the plane down. I was sitting on his right, rubbing the frost from the front window; trying to find an opening through the blinding snowstorm when suddenly the engine caught fire. Pa got up, strapped a parachute on me and told me to hold onto Jenny. I had just put my arms around her when he pushed us out of the plane. Seconds later we saw him crash into the mountain side, his airplane bursting into flames. My parachute didn't have a chance to open, even though I pulled hard on the release handle. I remembered it was only a short drop to the ground, I remembered seeing pine trees; and I remembered rolling over and over.

It was getting darker now, night was approaching; we still had no place to start a fire and warm ourselves. We took the parachute and made a canopy large enough for us to get out of the wind and snow. We tucked the loose flaps of the parachute under our bodies and held each other to stay warm. And we couldn't help thinking of poor Pa. He was gone and so was his airplane. He was proud of that plane, mostly because he helped build it. They finished production last year, it was on the 25th of June, 1925 and Mr. Lockheed gave Pa a plane of his own for doing such as good job. He had logged in over 400 miles and we were taking the plane to his sister's place in California. Aunt Elma has a ranch just outside of Fresno and Pa said her Uncle Joe created a space for a runway for our plane. Somewhere down on the south forty, they said. We were heading there and just had gotten clearance from Barstow to land. It was to be our last fuel stop when the unexpected snow storm began, turning abruptly into a blizzard which Pa said threw us off course.

I woke up with Jenny staring at me, her eye's wide open. Then very slowly she whispered, "You smell coffee, or am I crazy?" I pulled back the parachute and looked out into the bright sunshine and even brighter snow. The storm had debated and everywhere you look was white, blue, and dark evergreen. It was a beautiful morning, and there not twenty feet from us was a huge man sitting on a log; drinking coffee from a large mug. "Morning kids," he said, then added, "Names Bridger, and I'm about to make up a mess of flapjacks. You guys want some?"

We sure did, and began telling him our names and how we got here. "Well," he said, "I kind of figured that out. I was up there on the mountain when I saw your Pa push you out of the airplane. He was right in doing that, he saved your lives. Either the crash or the fire would have done him in anyways. It was lucky for you two that it was a short drop to the ground. Over there on my mule is a pack with soap and towels inside. Just beyond that rise is a small creek where you can wash up and clean yourselves. Meanwhile, I'll start the flapjacks."

We had heard of mountain men, and even of James Bridger; and we wondered if he was the one and the same. The bar of soap was made of pumice and washed the crime off our skin real good. We sat down on a log opposite him and watched him cook. He poured us both a cup of coffee, added a little water to cool it off a bit; then put a lump of sugar into each cup. It was the best coffee that I ever tasted, Jenny too. Then we laughed when he said that he'd bet us that this was the first time ever that we had coffee to drink. He was right. But his pancakes, what he called flapjacks; definitely were the best that we ever had… bar none. He used fat back, a type of bacon; to get the frying pan ready for the batter. He cooked two at a time, and when done; he placed them on a tin plate. Next he laid a piece of fried fat back on top, then poured maple syrup over all.

They were the best we have ever eaten. Jenny and I helped him clean up after breakfast and then we sat down on the log around the fire. "Well, Miss Jenny and Mr. Joe," he said, "This is the facts as I see them. We are in a section of the Rocky Mountains where very few men have seen, and only few have traveled. I hunt and trap here mainly because other people won't and don't. The nearest place I can think of that has a telegraph is a general store down along the Lower Platte. That's a river and is about four day's walking distance. After that, there's two months' worth of hiking down to the small mining town of Sagebrush. Now, the part that you probably don't want to hear is that I'm not going to leave this area until the spring thaw…which is about three or four months away." I looked at Jenny and knew she was about to cry, when he continued, "But what we will do right now, that is if it is okay with you two; is that we'll leave this spot and head for the general store. Once there, you can stay with Old Man Grimes if you a mind to; until we hear from your relatives. Either way, just thought you two should know the jest of it."

"Are you the Jim Bridger that we have read about?" asked Jenny. "Yes Missy, I'm the same," he said, then added, "I've been up here in these mountains for quite some time now. I originally was settled in old Tennessee, up in the Appalachians. Had me a wife, Little Feather was her name. Those were the days, full of fun and life. I used to drink white lightening with Davy Crockett, Jim Bowie too; over at Ike's General Store. Then Davy and Jim had to go to Texas, sort of a promise that they made to some man named Austin. Anyhow, Davy and Jim both died there at a mission called the Alamo. After that, Little Feather and I packed up and headed up here. Now, let's get started over to the general store. And by the way, call me Jim!"

The weather held up and it was a pleasant hike downhill to the general store, even though we had to camp out under the stars for two nights. Jim had laughed at us when he realized that it was a good thing we were heading for the store because we had eaten all the flapjack mix he had. Coffee and sugar was about gone too, he said. Then about an hour away from the store, Jim took out his long Sharp's rifle and shot a huge elk. He taught Jenny and I right then and there the proper way to skin an elk, even showing us what best meat parts to cut away whole and which ones to cut into small pieces for stewing. He even showed us what should be thrown away and buried.

When we got to the store, Jim shouted out from the landing on the porch, "Give us a hand, we got a lot of elk to take inside." Three men appeared and started to take off the two large bundles from the mule. We all went inside and Jim introduced us to Mr. Grimes and his two sons, John and Mathew. Mr. Grimes asked if we had eaten yet, and Jim said no. He then asked Mr. Grimes if he would get the griddle going, for he wanted to cook up the internals he had kept for later this morning. "I'll do that for you Jim," Mathew said, and went over to the stove and broke out a huge frying pan and several tin plates. John volunteered to make a fresh pot of coffee, and Jim just nodded his head in approval. "Jenny and Joe," Jim said. "There's a bath tub out in the storeroom. You two can take turns taking a bath and there are some clothes in the back you can change into if you want to wash what you're wearing.   And I just put two full buckets of hot water inside the room, so pick straws or whatever and get cleaned up. You both should be finished by the time breakfast is ready."

Breakfast was truly a mountain man's breakfast, one that I will never forget for the rest of my life. Mathew pan fried the elk heart, liver, and several slices of the small cuts of meat. Mr. Grimes ground up two small shoulders and made creamed beef, using milk from the cow he kept inside his small barn. He also said later that he was going to smoke the two big elk legs and some of the brisket. Jim found some root vegetables in the downstairs storeroom and made a stew. John made buttermilk biscuits from flour and eggs he brought from town. And they all used bacon fat that Mr. Grimes had on hand.

Jenny had taken a bath first and when I finally came out, breakfast was ready. They all wanted to know how Jenny and I came to be here and Jim was more than glad to tell the story, with Jenny and me chirping in from time to time to keep the story straight. We were still hurting from the death of our Pa but we were glad to have everyone say that he was a real hero, doing the right thing; even it is cost him his own life. Then the talk got around to going down the mountain, and it was then that Jenny and I realized that they weren't talking about just one mountain; but a mountain range called the Rockies. Like Jim told us before, it would take almost two months just to walk down to the closest town. And since the mountain passes were snowed in, it wouldn't be until spring thaw that we could even begin to make the trip.

The next day, Mr. Grimes telegraphed my Aunt in Fresno. It took a week, but we finally got a reply. After hearing of our accident, she agreed with Jim that the best recourse was to wait until spring since there wasn't anything they could do. My Aunt also asked if Jim would look out for us until then, and that she would repay him for our room and board. Jim laughed out loud at that, then had Mr. Grimes telegraph her that we would be just fine. He also told her that he had gone up to the accident sight and buried our Pa up on the Timberline, at the base of Twin Peaks just before daylight, then he found us.

That afternoon with the snow coming down in large, heavy flakes; we sat around the stove. Mr. Grimes put a large kettle of elk stew on top of the steel grate, telling everyone that the longer it cooks the more tender the meat. John and Mathew were sharpening their knives, and John asked Jim if it was alright if he skinned Jenny and me and made jerky out of us. Jim said no, then added that Jenny was too skinny. Jenny then said, "Just how old are you guys?" Jim spoke up first, saying "I don' rightly know. You see, I was born just after George Washington became President of these here United States. As a kid living in the back hills of the

Appalachians, I learned a lot about hunting from Davy Crockett. Knife throwing I learned from Jim Bowie and telling tall tales, well Old Ike up on Granite Mountain; you could write several books of his stories. There is one story, however, that Old Ike liked to tell that was true."

"I was there when Davy Crockett killed himself a bear when he was only three years old. You see, a couple of Indians gave Davy a tomahawk one day when Davy and his Pa were inside Ike's General Store. Ike had just sold his last two pouches of tobacco to Davy's Pa. They were about to leave when his Pa said to wait a minute, and gave them one of his tobacco pouches; asking nothing in return. It was his Pa's way. Well, one of the Indians felt compelled to return the favor and gave young Davy his tomahawk. It was about a week later when Davy went out back behind his Pa's house with the tomahawk to practice throwing. He drew a circle on a cottonwood tree and practice throwing the tomahawk from a distance. He kept throwing and kept on missing too, because his Pa and I were standing right there and didn't say a word…just watching. Finally, Davy walked over to his throwing spot. He took his time, aiming very carefully at that circle; then reaching way back he threw the tomahawk with all his might. Well, that tomahawk flew right past that cottonwood and into a blueberry bush. All of a sudden we heard a loud cry, and then silence. We rushed over to the bush and I pulled back the shrub looked down on a small bear cub lying on the ground; the tomahawk imbedded in the side of his head. I watched Davy for a couple of days while his Pa took out after the mother, him telling Davy that it must be done or the mother would turn mad. The small cub I took deep into the woods and buried the body. And that story is true, because like I said; I was there."

Jenny still wanted to know, and kept asking about our ages. It turned out that Mathew was 19 and John had just turned 21. Jenny said she was 13 and that I was an old, at 14. Mr. Grimes just shrugged his shoulders and told Mathew and John to clean up, just to change the subject. "You kids help too," he said, "since it seems we got company until spring."

The next day Jim took us over to a hidden lake where he said he had several beaver traps. It had stopped snowing, and he said he wanted to check his traps. Mathew came running up the path we had just made in the snow and said, "Jim, you forget your poles?" They both laughed then and Jenny and I realized that this was Jim's excuse for going fishing. At the lake, Jim showed us how to rig a fishing line with a small hook for a worm or maggot, and how to attach a cork about three feet from the hook so it would float on the surface of the lake. Then he said, "Keep an eye on the cork, let the fish strike, then when he strikes again, pull on the line to set the hook, then pull him in. Got that?" "Jenny just had to ask, "What if he is a she?" Jim just smiled and said, "Then give her to me. I like all the girls!!" We all had to laugh at that. Turned out that just before dusk, we had pulled out ten trout and four small mouth bass. It was as Jim had said, "Just enough dinner for us all." On the way back, Jim found some wild carrots and pulled out the larger ones; keeping the smaller ones in the ground until next time. "These," Jim said, "And some potatoes fried in bacon fat will be good with the fish."

Those winter months flew by after that, with Jim, John and Mathew taking us up and down the mountains. We learned about beaver, fox, wolverines, mountain lions, deer, and elk and just about every critter we encountered. Mathew had killed three mountain lions and with the help of Mr. Grimes, who was also an experienced taxidermist; and mounted all three for sale in town in the spring. And Mr. Grimes had gotten fond of Jenny, teaching her how to cook biscuits on top of the stove; even how to make beef jerky and everything else she inquired about. We were becoming a family and we didn't even realize it.

It was on a Sunday morning when John and I were standing outside the cabin drinking coffee when John said, "When Jim falls on his ass, its spring thaw." I watched as Jim was walking down the slope beside the cabin with Jenny, and sure enough; down he went. He approached the cabin and started walking up the stairs onto the porch. He looked at John and said, "Not a damn word, understand!" We started packing for our trip into town, and according to Jim; that was going to be tomorrow morning.

It took us five weeks before we reached Sagebrush, with the only street in the middle of town covered with mud a foot deep from the melting snow. One bank, one barber shop, one hotel, one general store; and four saloons encompassed the entire town. We had a telegram waiting for us at the hotel. It was from my Aunt in Fresno. She said she was sorry, but with her losing my Uncle Joe in the war in Europe; she was unable to send for us. She further said that she lost her farm and had to spend what savings she had. She was now living with her mother and several boarders at her mother's rooming house in Fresno. Everyone was having a hard time, with the depression and all; she said at the end of her letter.

Mr. Grimes took us into the dining area of the hotel and we sat down. He passed the telegram around so everyone to read. Then John said, "What's the problem?" Jim stood up and said, "There is no problem we can't fix. Let's go." He led us out of the hotel, across the muddy street, and into a saloon. There we found the Circuit Judge playing cards. Apparently Jim knew the judge and said, "Kyle, please read this telegram." After a few moments judge looked at us, and then asked Jim if he was willing to accept guardianship. Jim said yes, then the Judge looked right at Jenny and me. After a few moments, he said, "I believe you two have a small problem here, but I can resolve it right here and now if you two are willing to have Jim Bridger as your guardian until your eighteen years of age." We replied, "Of course, he is like our Pa already!" Then the judge wrote the same on my aunt's telegram and the judge signed it.

Everyone at the table just sat there and didn't say a word. I found out later that most folks thought Jim Bridger was long dead, a legend that stories were still told of around camp fires. Then the judge looked at our new Pa, and said, "Thanks Jim, not many men would take on this kind of responsibility. You and old man Grimes take care of them and make sure that they get some schooling." Then he hesitated a minute and counted out four hundred dollars off the card table and handed it to Jim. "Get them some new clothes and shoes before you go back up. That money is from the state of Nevada so don't worry about paying it back. And a couple of school books, too!"

Well, that's how Jim Bridger became our Pa. We spent summers at Jim's place on the lakeshores of Lake Tahoe. There was a general store there and Jenny got herself a summer job. She made a dollar and twenty-five cents an hour working there. Mr. Hopkins taught her all about being a cashier and handling general merchandise, keeping books too! During the winter months we went back up to Twin Peaks to stay with Mr. Grimes and his sons. It was went Jenny turned eighteen that she and John got married. They moved over to Carson City and started their own general store. Jim had given them a whole big bag of gold he had stashed away under his cabin. Mathew and I got called up by the Army and shipped out to Florida to join up with Teddy Roosevelt and his Rough Riders. There was a war going on with Cuba and we were pressed into service. It was at San Juan that Mathew lost his arm, was discharged, and had gone back to Twin Peaks. Old Man Grimes died soon afterwards, and two days later, so did Jim. We buried them side-by-side, next to my Pa up on the mountain. The entire town of Sagebrush turned out, which I was glad, for it took twelve men just to carry Jim up that mountain. And Jim left his cabin to me, and I couldn't believe my fortune. He had always told me that if I ever needed any money, just to look under his cabin

After I finished my two years with the Army, I returned to Twin Peaks. Mathew was doing just fine, got himself a wife now, with baby on the way. I went down the mountain to Lake Tahoe. Jim had left me his cabin and well, I just wanted to get away for a while. I had money from the Army, they giving me twenty-five dollars and certificate of Honorable Service; and they even had it framed. One morning when I was fishing on the bank of the lake, I remember what Jim had said and went back to the cabin. Over the fireplace were a couple of lanterns and took them with me down into the cellar. I couldn't believe my eyes, there was gold everywhere. Two bags full of gold nuggets were near a table and looking around it became very obvious that Jim had built his cabin right on top of a gold mine. The dirt basement had gold nuggets embedded in the walls as well as the floor. I sealed the trap door leading down to the cellar, removing only one bag of gold. I remembered what he said, "Take only what you need, spend wisely, or you will lose everything." I took the gold to the Bank of Nevada at Lake Tahoe and placed it in a safety deposit box.

Every now and then I took only what I needed from the box, and dealt only with the bank's manager. It took a while, my bringing a bag or two at a time to the bank. The bank's manager knew I was rich, and before long I became his boss; with him teaching me the ins and outs of the business. He had known Jim Bridger and became a good friend as well as an assistant manager. And my bank grew after a while, with over a thousand accounts being added per month. I knew people wanted a bank that extended loans and never foreclosed on your home just because you were having problems. And when the Feds came to find out why I was doing so well, they were taken aback when they walked into vault and saw several large boxes with over four million in gold. We came up with the idea of having people know that there money was "secured from loss"…and the idea was eventually copies by the federal banks.

From time to time I sent money to Jenny and Mathew, they always suspecting but never knowing exactly where it came from. John finally came off the mountain and accepted a job from me as co-president of the bank. It would have been what Jim would have wanted and John knew that too. And it was John's idea to remodel my office and turn it into an employee's lounge. My office, well it's right across from John's. And as you enter our bank, I'm on the right and John is on the left…with the teller's only a short step ahead at the back. You should see the look on peoples' faces when they enter the bank and asks to speak with the bank's manager. "You just passed them," they would reply. And one more thing, we don't wait until exactly nine o'clock to open the doors. You arrive early…and I will personally let you in!

And in the center of our city, I had erected a statue of Jim Bridger, our towns' founding father. He was a mountain man of fame and fortune, a man as famous as Davy Crockett and Jim Bowie, or Daniel Boone. And I was proud to be called his son. And lastly, this Christmas I'll be going over to Jenny's house. I'm bring the elk and John's bringing trout he caught up in the high county, right at the Timberline.

The One Armed Bandits

It was pouring cats and dogs as I ran from beneath the tree and straight into the pub. Why a pub is located this deep in the forest I'll never know, but was mighty glad it was here when a tree trunk not ten yards from me was struck by lightning. I was coming from a BP station over on A321, my car had broken down; and the guy there was kind enough to tell me of this pub…being not too far off.

There was a little old man standing behind the bar, and as I sat down on the stool in front of him; I asked him how long this pub has been here. "This pub was my father's, and his father's before him; and before him I've been told that it belonged to a man named Charles Squirrel," he said with pride. "Is that why the squirrel on the sign outside is pink?" I asked, for I had noticed the unusual sign as I crossed the path. "No sir," he replied, "that was my daughter's doing. You see, the squirrel used to be white; and my daughter thought it would be more appropriate to change the name of the pub from "Squirrel's" to "The Red Squirrel". So I let her have her way and she had her cousin change the color to red. It wasn't supposed to rain that evening, but with the red paint still damp; the red color bled into the white…and the bloody squirrel turned pink."

To change the subject away from the sign, I asked, "Is this the same pub that Robin Hood used to frequent?" "It sure is," he said with visible pride, then added, "and that old dart board in the back room with the arrow in the bulls-eye is Robin's own. I was told that it was on a rainy evening like this that Robin was playing darts with Little John. Some Berkshire bloke came over and bet Robin two quid that he couldn't put an arrow in the bulls-eye from across the room. Now Robin was of a mind as to not to disappoint anyone, so he set his playing arrows down on the bar; picked up his bow and an arrow from his quiver…and made a neat shot from 40 feet away…dead center in the red bulls-eye. Everyone present had to laugh at that because we knew he was referring to Robin's darts, what some call arrows. And with Robin being a bit of a jester himself, he gave him his due."

"Tell you what," I said, the continued, "here's a pound note, why don't you pour yourself and I two large pints of ale and we will discuss this dart tournament you have here on the last Friday of every month." He went over to the back bar and picked up a large clipboard with several schedules attached. Then he motioned me to join him at a nearby table and we both sat down. "Oops!" he said, then got back up and went back to the bar. He poured a large pitcher of dark ale and grabbed two glasses on his way back to the table. Then he said, "The pound note will go into our dart leagues pool, and the ale is on me." I then introduced myself and shook hands with the jolly little fellow. I don't know why, but I liked him immediately; for he was the kind of man that enjoyed life…the kind of man you could call a friend. I told him that I was the manager of a dart league over in Glen Hollow, and we play out of the Green Frog Pub. We heard of an upcoming tournament being held here, and with the bold statement… "Come play with the best…The One Armed Bandits".

As he poured us another round of ale, I asked "I also understand that the tournament is open to all challengers. Is that correct?" He just laughed a bit, the said, "From days of old, the men and women of Sherwood have always accepted challenges from those who are willing." "Very good," I responded, then asked, "I suppose the rules of darts in your shire would be the same as ours?" "Good that you brought that up," he said, then continued, "Let me go over them just to make sure. First, we play "301". We have no limit as to how many teams complete. There is no entrance fee, but the teams are limited to four players.

Now let's say there are four teams competing. The teams that will complete with each other are initially chosen by the Captain of each team, lagging for the bulls-eye. The Captain with the nearest arrow to the bulls-eye goes against the Captain with the second nearest arrow, and so forth. So for example, team one may play against team four; then team two against team three. The completion begins by a member of each team lagging for the center. That team will throw first, with members of both teams alternating players. After the end of one game of 301, the winning team buys the losing team a pint of their favorite drink. Then the next two teams play, then the next two. The Captains of each winning team will draw numbers from a bowl. The team drawing number one will play against number two, etc.

All teams will continue playing in that manner until there are only two winning teams are left. Then they will complete against each other in one game of 301, and the team to reach zero first will be declared the winner. The Championship trophy will be awarded to the winning team, and they will have their teams name displayed on the trophy for prosperity. My pub, being the tournament sponsor, will donate a check in the amount of 150 pounds to St. Catherine's orphanage. Next month, I believe, the Pig in the Sky will hold the tournament and they will select a charity of their choosing."

"Well," I said, "those rules are almost identical to ours, except that we are near the city of Berkshire, and being within alcohol taxation, we charge more for drinks…but we also give a bigger donation. But as you know, it is for charity and good will that we have these tournaments. Now tell me," I added, "just what are these one armed bandits? I haven't seen any slot machines anywhere inside." "You'll soon discover…" he said, as he was interrupted by a couple of patrons who had just entered. He became busy and I left his fine old pub, but not before examining the walls. These walls really were old and worn…imagine…Robin Hood!

The day of the tournament finally arrive and I had my four players siting in the back seats of my van. I looked back, what a view. Although the year was 1947, I couldn't comprehend why my four girls; glamour models one and all… weren't married. They loved playing darts, and they loved playing in dart tournaments. And as far as marriage, they told me, "In time mate, in time!" I noticed the front of their shirts…no, not that kind of front. But the logo that they had chosen for their team… "The Dart Knights". And even though my wife and I were their coaches and sponsors, they really didn't need much coaching…all were very good players.

Cindy (my youngest daughter, age 18) could hit the bulls-eye four out of every five throws. Cathy (my second youngest daughter, age 20) could hit the bulls-eye three out of every five throws. Wendy (my oldest, age 22) well, if you get her upset at you, then run like hell…she really is that good. Our fourth player is our neighbor's daughter. Her real name is Maxwell, but we call her Maxi for short. She is a lovely girl 19 who can actually claim Little John as her great, great, great…grandfather! The Priory at St. Michaels has the documentation to prove her claim which I have actually seen. Little John, I am told; was an outstanding dart player…so is Maxi!

As we entered the Pink Squirrel, my wife gave a cold look at several young men who started to whistle at our girls. There were a total of four teams present: "The Mulligan's" from the village of Gloustershire, "The Bulls-Eyes" from Somerset, and "The Dart Knights," of course. The team that made me really take notice was the team from Berkshire…"The One Armed Bandits".

These were four beautiful young ladies, with ages I guessed were similar to my own team's ages; with only one very noticeable distinction. As we watched them warm up, I was amazed to watch how good they were. More amazing was their attitudes and sparkle in their eyes. You could see that they were having a good time and enjoying themselves. "You know dear," my wife said, "those One Armed Bandits only have one arm!" I discovered later that they had been involved in a terrible avalanche in the Swiss Alps; their train thrown down into a deep ravine. They were among the few who survived and met one another during rehabilitation at a hospital in Bern. In the two years they were together they good became friends, and were encouraged to exercise as often as possible…and they chose darts.

The tournament was close, and the floor of the pub was getting soaked from ale being spilled. Yet everyone was having a good time and finally the last two teams were announced. The Dart Knights would play against the One Armed Bandits. Wendy threw against Jennifer and won the lag, our team would throw first. As my wife and I were waiting for the players to start, the bartender came over with fresh pints. It was then that we found out that he was the pub's owner and his name was Clink. I just had to ask, "Why do they call you Clink? He just smiled and raised his glass up to mine, and "clink"!

The players were good, on both teams; and the scores showed it. I was watching as Jennifer was walking up to the throw line, stopped; and came directly in front of me. "Thank you," she said. And when she saw the surprised look on my face, she added, "I guess Cathy didn't tell you that we are all spending the night at your place and to tell you to not to forget to call ahead for pizzas. My wife's eyes opened wide when she said, "Twelve extra, extra large pizzas: three pepperoni only, two cheese only, two pepperoni and mushrooms, and three combinations." I couldn't speak, but my wife said, "Not a problem sweetheart, now get in there as do your best." And she did, and when Wendy passed her walking up to the throw line; she stuck her tongue out at Jennifer. Then they both started laughing. Clink came over with a large pint of ale for me. "On the house," he said and started laughing, then he added, "I overheard the order." I wasn't paying attention to him... I was still trying to figure out how much it would cost me!

The crowd in the pub was beginning to quiet down and it was obvious that the tournament was coming to an end. I watched as Wendy smiled as she walked up to the throw line, exactly eight feet from the bristle board. She had a score of 251, yet she needed fifty points; and she had to double-out with her last dart to win the game. I watched as she held her breath, and then she made the shot that brought the house down; she hit the bulls-eye...dead center, a double-twenty five for the game. Even if Robin Hood had been here, I don't think he could have done better.

There were three vans in our caravan on the road heading to our home, the large trophy in back of the last van with Clink. He told my wife he hadn't had pizza in some time…and since he brought along two large kegs of pilsner, it was party time! I was still trying to figure out what all those pizzas would cost, when my wife started to laugh and said, "Stop it dear, it's only money!"

The Man from Brindisi

My Aunt had suggested that my Grandfather Tito
would be a good candidate for a story, that is; if I were
willing to travel all the way to Italy. I was running out
of material for a good story, for like many other young
aspiring authors: every subject, theme, or farfetched
ideas were already used, or abused to the extreme. I was
looking for something that was original, something that
no one else could possibly think of…something real!

With my Aunt's assistance, i.e. money; I was onboard
the next flight to Naples. From there my Uncle Luigi
would pick me up and we would drive cross country.
Uncle Luigi said that my Grandfather Tito was waiting
for me, for he had never seen his grandson. He
apparently was told everything about me, for in my
family; everyone knows about everyone. And he was
anxious to get started on my book, the one about him;
the one about a man from Brindisi.

"So, whatta you wanna know kid?" Uncle Tito said. I
was stilling trying to overcome the fact that he had just
kissed me on both of my cheeks…yuck! I sat down at
the table across from him, looked directly into his eyes;

and said "I came here to write a book about you. And what I want to hear is everything. Start from the beginning, from the time you were born; and go slow…I'm a writer, not a secretary. And take your time, my Zia says you were one hell of a man in your day; and that's the story I am looking for. "Okay," Uncle Tito said, then added, "You just sit there next to that machine of yours. And bring over that bottle of vino, and some salami too!"

"My story starts when I was born, not too far from here as a matter of fact. Bari was a small village then, about ten or twelve families. My parents lived on a farm and we provided milk for the entire village. We owned five cows back then and it was one morning while my Mama was milking… I was born. She was squatting down, squeezing the cow's teats; filling the bucket with milk. She moved over a bit, setting herself over a big pile of cow shit; and grunted. And I was born, landing right in the middle of that pile of shit. She cut my cord with her teeth, then sat me down on a stool; then she told me to milk the other cow. Well, at least that's the story as I was told. And to this day I can still squeeze a cow's teat with the best of them.

Anyways, life on the farm was typical of those days; the year was 1901 when I was born. No one had much of anything then, and we sold whatever extra we had to travelers on the road; or bartered with other families for things we needed. For example, one family raised pigs, another grew corn and wheat; and still another raised chickens and sold eggs. I still remember when I was six years old and it was my job to go over to the chicken farm and ask for six eggs: two were for my Papa's breakfast, two were for cooking, and two eggs my Mama broke into a cup…just the yolks. She stirred the egg yolks with a little sweet wine, and that was for me to drink. The left over egg whites she mixed in with flour, sweet butter and milk; then with the dough she flatted and fried like a donut.

Like was good then, and although we had no schools nearby, the Senora at the chicken farm taught us how to read, and write a little. She also taught us how to add Lira so we wouldn't get cheated by the travelers on the road. My total education, if counted in years like they do today, would probably be the third grade. When I was eight, my Papa stopped sending me to the chicken farmer's wife, and had me working with the wheat and corn farmer. But he sent me back to the chicken farm to clean out the chicken coops, he needed the fertilizer. And when he had a field of tall corn, he had me help harvest the corn. Then we had to cut the stalks down to the roots, lay them to dry in the sun; and then tied them in bales for the horses and cows to feed on during the winter.

And I remember one winter when I turned twelve and everyone with a patch of land needed help to plow the ground. That was the first time I saw ma Pa laugh when there was people around. They wanted me to plow, but the plow was bigger than I was. So they put me to work walking in front of the plow, picking up large stones; then carrying them over next to the road to make a stone fence.

The following winter, on my birthday in fact, the Italian Army came around our village looking for men to fight against the Austrians. My Papa couldn't go because of his right leg, he limped all the time. Mama said that I was two years old when two cows pinned him against a stall inside the barn, his leg was crushed somewhat; but he eventually was able to walk some. My Mama started crying when the Captain said, "We'll take him." It was the 28th of November, 1915, and I had just turned thirteen.

There is not much to tell you about the war, expect that it is something that you either die, or live through; if you're lucky. And I was lucky, for from the time I arrived at the Austrian front; I was assigned as a cook's helper. I scrubbed pot and pans mostly, but when we had potatoes; I was in charge of peeling them. And when we found a stray cow that was in need of milking, they were amazed that I knew how to milk one. Goats too! My real name was Giuseppe but they called me "Tito" because I was real good with a cow's teats.

My luck soon ran out, and during the Austrian counteroffensive of 1917, our unit pulled back and I was handed a helmet and a rifle. I was with the 1st Regiment when we regrouped and attacked the Austrians again, and again, and again. My platoon drove through the lines and deep into Austrians territory.   After several days, we overcame them. The fighting ended on the 28th of November, and I had just turned sixteen. I was promoted to Sergeant and was awarded the Infantry Cross, the Italian Service Cross; and a Purple Heart for being wounded under fire. The fact is, I was shot in the ass. To this day I don't know who shot me, for my platoon was constantly charging ahead; but I sure would like to find out. You wanna see my bullet hole?

They gave us leave and I was lucky enough to be relocated to Bari, my Captain having some pull. He told my Papa that it was not often that you see a sixteen year old Sergeant with combat ribbons! I also was lucky that my barracks was only five miles from our farm and spent my off hours at the farm. But then the Captain gave me my own platoon, and I didn't get to go home too often. He also gave me several green recruits to make into soldiers.

The cooks at our camp loved me, for I had those recruits spend at much time peeling potatoes as they spent on the rifle range. These were Italian kids, all of them from large cities; so I knew they already knew how to fight. What I was looking for were guys that would stick together, guys who could throw a potato as well as a hand grenade. And every single one of them was taller than me, and of course; they thought they were tougher than me too! But we never had a chance to find out.

Exactly fifteen months after my return to Bari that we found ourselves involved in another war, this time with Germany…with Austrian also back in the conflict, fighting on their side. We were not the first to arrive at the front, but we certainly were the most welcomed; for the 2nd Brigade was getting their butts kicked. At Algermina.the Germans had their men pinned down from inside an old church. They had the high ground, with the church overlooking the countryside and our troops. The 2nd Brigade was running low on ammunition when we arrived. I took my platoon on a flanking maneuver and came up behind the church. I led the way and my platoon soon learned why I was called the Italian version of GI Joe. Crawling on my stomach most of the way, I led those green kids straight into the courtyard of the church. Several grenades later, we stormed the enemy from two sides, and continued our attack until we had secured the church. Although we had killed over forty Germans, my platoon had only suffered one casualty.

We regrouped with our company and surged ahead towards the newly established front. It was during this skirmish that I got shot again, and yes; it was in the ass. Only this time, it was the other cheek. My Commander wanted to know how it was that I got shot in the ass again, since he knew I was always moving forward; meeting the enemy head on. I had no answer, but I got another medal and a week's leave at Lake Como, our Army's staging area.

Some leave, for I just laid on my cot at the camp for the entire time. And yes, I was lying face down! I was lying down too when our regiments General entered the hospital and gave me and several other soldiers the Croce de Guerra, or War Cross. It was my third, and I had just turned eighteen. The General also promoted me to Sergeant Major. I asked my Commander why did had skipped Sergeant First Class rating, and he just laughed at me. Later I found out that the General and he had discussed giving me a battlefield commission, but the Commander said no; he owed me a favor. The Germany Army was notorious for aiming their bullets at officers.

Several weeks later I found myself with my new company, consisting of four platoons; numbering 640 men. I was the smallest of the lot...but I was their leader. During inspections one morning I overheard someone asking if that little shit was really that tough. The response made me smile, for the man said that he really didn't want to find out; for he could see that the ribbons on my chests said it all: four purple hearts and three Silver Medals. And everyone knew that you only receive a Silver Medal when you receive at least four War Cross's, and those you earn by being in the trenches. I walked to the end, turned around, and then started up the second row of men. Then I stopped in front of a new recruit, who I knew was part of the Ragazzi del 99; all seventeen year olds who had been called up by the government. I stopped in front of a kid who barely looked seventeen, gave him a little smile and then told him to report to the Cook.

The following Monday, our entire battalion was back in the trenches; but going east this time. It was around noon were we found ourselves breaking through the Austrian front at Sacile. I lost quite a few men and had to hold our position overnight. But the next day, with reinforcements arriving; we soon had over 300,000 Austrians as prisoners of war. We made several camps with fortified enclosures for the prisoners and waited for orders. We believed we were close to the end, with the Austrians soon surrendering. Our Commander said several of our platoons were still advancing and for us to hold our position. A week later, on 3 November, the war was over with a formal armistice being signed."

The old man looked at his empty glass and said, "Over in the corner there is another bottle of wine. And while you are there, look on the wall." I crossed the room and picked up the bottle and did exactly as he had asked...I looked at the wall. My lower jaw just fell down...I was flabbergasted. I mean, no...wrong words; and no words could express what I was looking at. The large photograph was of Tito and his company, with him in the center. At five feet tall, he was indeed the shortest man in the company. Then, surrounding the photograph, I counted twenty-one medals he had earned; including the World War I Victory Medal.

"Hey kid," Uncle Tito said, "the bottle of vino...prego!" He poured himself another glass of wine and continued, "After the armistice, I headed home to be with my family. Giovanna, the chicken farmer's daughter, had grown up to become a beautiful woman; with teats that were really big. After a few months at home, her father had begun to make daily visits to our home to ask about his daughter. 'What are your intentions?' he would ask me again and again. Finally my own father interjected with the announcement that I will never, ever forget. 'Well son,' he said to me, 'you have been plucking her more often than her chickens, isn't it about time you two got married?' I couldn't help myself, and before long all three of us were laughing. 'Maybe I could help you build an extra room behind your cottage,' the chicken farmer said. Let her set a date, I told them both; then opened a bottle of brandy I had bought in Bari.

We toasted the engagement, we toasted the 1st Regiment; we toasted the new crop of wine…even the new calf. Hell, we toasted everything and everyone that evening; sometimes twice. It wasn't until the next morning when we woke up in the living room that we discovered we had finished four bottles of brandy. I thought that I heard my own Mama in the others room, with Giovanna and her mother celebrating and giggling about her new finance, their engagement…and well, her wedding day!

I thought that I had been out of the Army for good with the war being over, but the following month my old Commander came by for a visit. 'I've taken command of the Bari encampment,' he said, 'and that you might like to visit their sometimes, after all, you are still in the Army.' I had no idea, hell, I had just turned nineteen and had spent six years in the Army…wasn't that enough! 'Times are tough,' he said, 'and we lost a lot of good men over in Austria…and I need good men to help me train new recruits…I need you! And besides, Master Sergeant's receive a good income; you can spend weekends at home…and I'll even give you a month's furlough any time you want.' I wanted to talk to Giovanna first, but he added, 'How many War Crosses have your earned?' "Twelve," I responded. Then he said, 'We need to promote you to Senior Master Sergeant of the Command…in short, the base will be yours. How does that sound son?'

I couldn't pass that up and immediately said, 'Yes sir, I'll be there on Monday.' Giovanna might be upset, but both our families would be better off. We could use the base infirmary, commissary and clothing store. Even the base barber shop we could use any time we wanted. But more important, both our fathers wouldn't have to work in the fields any longer, my pay would be enough to see us through. So, on my 20th birthday, I stood at parade with our battalion: Four Class Alfa Platoons and three recruit companies. I became the senior enlisted man on base and our Commander introduced me as such in front of the entire brigade. We were at full dress parade, and everyone wore there medals which they had earned during the wars. Photographs were taken and eventually I brought home a photograph of the entire brigade, one for each family. 'Who's the little man standing there with all those medals?' Giovanna's papa asked. Then he recognized me and sat down. 'Damn', he said, 'I never knew you were a war hero.' 'I'm not,' I replied, 'only a soldier who was lucky enough to marry a farmer's daughter before her father shot me!' We all had to laugh at that.

Several years had passed and Giovanna and I had two sons and added four more cows to our herd. I was lucky enough to have a couple of Master Sergeants who were good at their jobs which enabled me to spend more time at home. I had just turned twenty-seven and was given another star for my uniform. Our Commander was impressed with our training, for every time he passed a few soldiers he overheard them cussing and calling me all sorts of bad names. I apparently was the meanest son-of-a-bitch they ever came across. But I knew as well as my Commander, when the fighting starts; they all will be covering my back.

Germany was now stirring trouble in northern Europe. A man called Hitler was coming to power, and many countries which bounded Germany were falling under his control. War wasn't too distant, and my Commander knew it… smelled it. He ordered me to increase bayonet training, close order hand-to-hand combat, and to spend each day on the rifle range. The grenade range too, he said as an afterthought. Then he said to requisition as much ammunition as possible, and not to forget foods of all kinds; including dry meats. Lastly, he said I know we will be called, we are the 1st Regiment; our reputation tells it all…we are the best!

Then he told me to go home, and handed me my discharge papers. Then he said he had amended them to include a retirement pension. You have done enough for Italy.... God bless you!"

"Well kid," Uncle Tito said, "that's your story. I'm afraid I haven't much else to add, for since my discharge I have been taking care of both our farms here in Bari. Your Grandmother had passed away several years ago, right after both our sons were killed in action in Africa. They had volunteered for the French Foreign Legion, wanting to follow in my footsteps. It was at Tangiers when they were killed. They were assisting men and women who were displaced by the war. It was a car bomb, they said. I buried them both here in Bari, next to their mother. The following day I departed for home. My aunt wondering why, and when I got there I told her...Uncle Tito has had enough of war.

It's been twenty years now, and both my aunt and uncle are gone. I found this story among many others that I had shelved. Then I sat down, opened a bottle of wine; and remembered him. You see, my Uncle Tito was a hero, a son, a husband, and a father. But most of all, he was a man from Brindisi.

Toby

It was six o'clock in the morning when I saw Toby for the first time. He was a short little guy, almost four feet tall; and a noticeable limp due to his having one leg shorter than the other. He had a job across the street at the OK Corral, an old barn and stable that Wyatt had converted into a saloon. They finished just before Christmas, the year being 1889, and Toby was given a job that nobody wanted… cleaning those brass jugs that men spat into. Jugs they called "Spittoons".

It probably wouldn't have been too bad, if more men had better aim. But this is Tombstone, Arizona, and Boot Hill is full of men who couldn't shoot straight; with or without tobacco. Toby received ten cents for each brass spittoon he cleaned and polished, and every morning, come rain or shine; he had ten spittoons to clean.

Toby's Ma worked at the OK Corral, night shift being the only available shift; but it paid for their one room she and Toby shared. Toby's Pa was long gone, and rumored to be buried in Boot Hill; but Toby never could find his grave marker. The one thing that Toby's Pa left him was an old watch, the kind that train conductors use. It wasn't gold, being made out of tin; but it worked. And on the backside of the casing were a series of marks and numbers. Toby showed it to Wyatt one day, but he just shrugged his shoulders and spit into a freshly cleaned and polished spittoon on the floor; a good twenty feet away. Toby had to smile at that, at least it was a clean shot; not one that he had to use extra pumice to clean it with.

Early one morning Toby came to see me. Even though I was financially established, I worked part time as a lawyer. I just had arrived in Tombstone three days ago, being sent by my boss in Chicago to defend his sister's cousin; Ike Clayton. Wyatt was still upset with me over the trial. Not only did I get Ike Clayton a misdemeanor judgment, with Ike having to pay only ten dollars in court costs; I also got a misconduct judgment against Wyatt, with him having to pay three month's salary and do ninety hours of community service.

Toby brought over one of the spittoons he had cleaned, then the poor lad turned his head and coughed; he had a bad cold. He told me to turn the spittoon over and look at the base. I could easily see that it was a map, and on closer examination; of the territory around Phoenix. I asked him if there were any other spittoons with markings on the bottom as this one. He said only this one so far, then he scurried across the street to the saloon. A few minutes passed when I saw him coming back, carrying another spittoon. I compared the two and it appeared that this one was a continuation of the other. I then asked Toby to find me some black boot polish. I took out a clean sheet of paper from the small desk in the corner. If I was guessing correctly, the black polish should tell us more about the two maps.

Toby's Ma knocked on the door and entered my office a few minutes later, looking for Toby; she said. I told her that he had gone to get some black boot polish and he should return in a few minutes. She then sat down, and noticed one of the spittoons I had on the table, lying on its side. She looked closely then at the bottom and said, "I know that area, my husband Dutch used to take me there a few times for a picnic. "Your husband's name is Dutch?" I asked. "Yes," she replied, then said, "And I know what you are about to ask me next, is Dutch the same man who discovered all that gold on Superstition Mountain?" "Well, yes," I replied.

"Sorry," she responded with a smile, wrong Dutch! My husband would have told me, but he's dead now, buried up on Boot Hill; so they tell me. "You didn't attend his funeral?" I just had to ask. "No," she said, "For I work nights and sleep during the day. Besides, my husband treated my son and me like we were strangers, never really caring; never being around much. He spent most of his time up there on Superstition with his mule. I think he loved that mule of his more than he loved me, or his son. After he died, Toby and I went through his packs he carried on his mule. The only thing we found were these brass spittoons. It was because Toby had these that he was given the job cleaning them at the OK Corral...them cheapskates!"

Toby arrived with the boot polish and I asked him to go over to the saloon and bring back the rest of the spittoons. He looked at me like I was crazy, then I said, "Just empty the full ones out on the street as you come back. "By the way sir," Toby's Ma started to say, "I'm called Mildred, and you already know my son Toby." "Sorry," I replied, then added, "I've only been in town a few days, coming in for the Clayton trial; my name is Bat Masterson. You really don't go by Mildred?" I just had to ask her. "No," she replied with a bright smile, "most folks call me Millie, and you can too." "Millie," I said, "you don't know me, but I want you to believe that you can trust me; for I have an idea about these spittoons. I want you to go over to see Mr. Johnson and ask him to meet us at the bank. I know that it's Sunday, but tell him that Bat Masterson is doing the asking. He knows me and he still owes me a few favors from years gone by. Toby and I will meet you two at the bank, and by the way, stop by the Marshall's office and bring him along too."

They were already at the bank when Toby and I arrived with those spittoons, it took a while because I kept dropping them. "Tom," I said to the banker as I stepped inside his office, "thanks for coming on such short notice. But I think that this is important enough to have you and the Marshall here. I then asked Toby to hand each person a spittoon, a clean one if possible. "Now what," the Marshall said. "Take a close look at these spittoon and tell me what you think?" I asked. "Well," said Millie, "the brass is wearing off. "Millie," I said to her, "that's a very good observation, and you should know that brass contains only brass…it doesn't wear off. Someone had several coats of brass applied to these spittoons. Toby had done such a good job polishing these that he had polished the brass off in several places." Then the Marshall opened his mouth and very slowly whispered… "Gold!"

The next morning Millie, Tom and I were having breakfast at Millie's place, even though the kitchen was real small. But somehow she turned out a stack of flapjacks with maple syrup that was fit for a king. "Or a banker," Tom added. "I wanted us to meet here," I said, "because it's quiet." I then turned to Millie and said, "What Toby has discovered is enough to turn most men

into thieves, with some even going stark raving mad…
even committing murder. As you know, Tom and I
examined the bases of all ten spittoons and discovered
that three out of ten had maps inscribed on their bottoms.
All the maps centered on Superstition Mountain, near
Phoenix. What you don't know is that Toby had shown
me he watch this morning when I asked him if he knew
the time. He pulled out his watch and proudly said,
"Seven o'clock on the dot." Then he asked me if I knew
what the scratches on the back of his watch meant, with
my being a lawyer and all. Tom and I both agree that if
you compare the watch with the maps, they should pin
point the exact locations of Dutch's mines.

Then I reached into my brief case and took out the
paper that I had intended to use earlier. I then rubbed
black shoe polish on the base of one of the spittoons that
had a drawing of a map, and pressed down lightly on the
paper. I repeated the step with the other two spittoons. I
then set the papers aside to dry for a few minutes. "What
are you attempting to prove?" Millie asked. "You'll
see," I replied, then said, "just give it a few minutes to
dry." I had seen this type of map making during the war
with the south, and I knew I was on to something. The
key was the watch, for on the back you marked the
locations with a small "x", and the underneath one, put a
small "n" indicating the direction for North. Therefore,
the map and the corresponding watch was never kept in
the same location until necessary.

The boot polish was dry now, and I picked up a smaller piece of paper with the watch's imprint. I made sure that I wrote the compass point down also with a pencil, I then poked a small hole at each of the three large indentations, and one at the smaller one. "This is our template," I announced, then asked Millie to let me have some of her face powder. I sprinkled powder on the maps so I wouldn't smear the boot polish, then, one by one; I pressed the template over each map. Then with the pencil, I inserted the point into each hole of the template, and pressed hard. After completing all three maps, I asked Tom and Millie to pick up a map and blow the powder off the surface. I did the same with the third map. "Make sure the template in lined up north, and they lay it down the paper; and align the holes with the dark dots on the paper. "You see," I said, "on this map I have aligned the large holes over the large dots on the map, and they match perfectly. Now, I am going on press the pencil in the smaller hole, and make an "X". Then I removed the template, and the spot I marked should correspond to an entrance to a mine. Tom had fixed the location on one of the other maps, but the third had no reference points whatsoever. I turned to Millie and said, "It appears that Dutch has not only left you gold, but also two gold mines!"

The next several days were exciting for Toby, for the bank's president gave him and his Mom several thousand dollars. At least that was what Toby had told me, having rushed over to my office to tell me the good news. I asked Toby to wait in my office for a few minutes and then ran over to see my old friend, Tom; at the bank. I met Millie in front of the dress shop and grabbed her by the arm and said, "Let's go." Tom was rather defensive at first, but he came around to his senses what I said, "Tom, you're looking at the man who pulled you out of several scrapes at Miller's Landing during the war...remember! And I am the one who loaned you the money to start this bank, and I told you then that I can't stand a thief!" "Sorry Bat," he said, "but they have so much." "No they don't," I countered. "Now Tom," I demanded, "you tell Millie exactly how much money she has." "Okay," was his response, then he offered, "I took these over to the Assay's office to have them tested and weighed. Seven of the spittoons tested right at 98 percent pure mineral gold. The three spittoons with the maps etched on the bottom tested in at 65 percent. The Assayer got out his magnifying glass and took a real close look again at the one of the spittoons with the etching. Then he changed the chemical solution in his testing kit to test for Mayan gold. The results read: 100 percent pure Mayan gold."

I watched Millie and she sat down, not sure of what Tom was saying. Then Tom continued, "And by the way, in case you're wondering; Mayan gold is worth ten times that of our Arizona gold." I then told Tom to give Millie one of his saving deposit books. "If it is okay with you Millie," I suggested, "sell the bank the three spittoons made from Mayan gold, which at $150.00 an ounce, will give you just over sixty thousand dollars on deposit. The remaining spittoons we will have sent to the First National Bank at Denver to be put in a safety deposit box."

"How about you Bat?" she asked, then added, "Toby and I owe you so much." "As for me," I replied, "I own 51 percent of this bank and am the president of the First National in Denver. I also own several diamond mines in four states and one gold mine in Peru, plus other mining interests in Mexico. But the point is that I was only interested in helping you, and especially Toby. And I would be very grateful if you allow me to tag along when you decide to find the Lost Dutchman's mines on Superstition Mountain.

It's been ten long year now, and as you probably already guessed, Millie and I did get hitched. I had my best friend, Wyatt; stand in as my best man. And Toby, well he's doing just fine. I had a hunch early on that he only had a mild congestive condition, and I got him back on his feet. And I also had a doctor friend of my up in Denver do corrective surgery on his leg and now Toby walks better than I do. Last year, he made us both proud by graduating from Denver State University, receiving a Master's Degree in Geology. He told us he plans on going to Peru to check on several possible mineral sites, and I am going with him; so is Millie and Jenny. Jenny, well, she was a welcomed addition to our family a couple of years ago.

And I suppose you want to know about Dutch's mines, the famous Dutchman's Gold of Superstition Mountain…well sir, there still there. The maps he had made were correct, right on the money in fact, pointing out exactly to where Dutch had his oats stored…for his mule!

The Cross

It was about two years ago I guess, spring time too since my roses were starting to bloom; when little Jimmy started coming over to my workshop. I suppose we are neighbors since there is a single fence separating St. Catherine's parish orphanage and my backyard. But most of the children just throw rocks over the fence and call me names. But little Jimmy was different, he was curious as to what went on inside my shop. It was Father Mathias, the headmaster for St. Catherine's; who brought Jimmy over. The Father was also new to the school and took this opportunity to meet me.

I took them down the steps next to my one car garage behind the house that I had converted into a woodshop some forty years back. They were amazed at all the clocks, and the numerous portraits of trains, ships, even horses and cats of all kinds that I had cut out of quarter inch plywood. I also had dozens of Christmas ornaments hanging from the ceiling and lining the walls. Father Mathias asked me where my tools were, for all he had seen on the bench was a hand held tubular scroll saw and a hand held rotary drill. I also had my knife, a pair of plyers, and a small hammer lying there. Then he noticed my candles, for I had about twenty or so that I used to see by in the evenings.

Then it dawned on the good father that I worked for him, and he said, "You're Giuseppe, aren't you?" "Yes father," I replied, then added, "I take care of your backyard from time to time by tending to your flowers and vegetables. This morning I picked some Kale for your dinner this evening." The father looked puzzled, then said, "But I didn't notice your name on our payroll, how is that?" "Oh, I don't need money father, "I said, "Your sisters bring me soup or whatever extra you might have. And every Friday on bake day they bring me a fresh loaf of sourdough bread. It lasts all week, too!" I said with a smile.

Then he changed the subject, by asking, "What type of wood do you use?" "Oh, just about any type of plywood I can get." I responded, then added, "Mike at the lumber yard brought me some quarter inch birch plywood a year ago. I had no money to pay for it, so we bartered. I gave him a clock I had made and ever since then he keeps me supplied. He's a real nice fellow, Mike is."

Father Mathias left after a while, and I heard him talking to himself as he started down the walkway… "Amazing, simply amazing…and with no electricity too!" Little Jimmy stayed for a while, then asked if he could come by tomorrow. Of course I said yes, and told him to use the gate in the backyard; for it was closer and easier for him since he was using crutches. I knew about Jimmy, for the sisters had told me of him and all the other children they cared for. There were twenty-four children in total, ranging from the ages of 8 to 16. Jimmy was ten and he also had a sister who was 8 years old. They're parents were killed in an automobile accident and with no other home to go to, they ended up at St. Catherine's.

The next morning I woke up early, as I always do; at first light. I don't have an alarm clock, never needed one; my wife used to wake me up to go to work…but that was a long, long time ago. I dressed and went out to water the plants and hoe the soil between the rows of vegetables that I had planted. Then I heard someone call, "Giuseppe!" Right on time I thought, as I went out the back gate over to the parish kitchen where I always have morning coffee with Sister Maria. She said that yesterday's Kale soup was so delicious that she just had

to save me some. And she put a big square of corn bread
on top of the soup pot for me to take too. Jimmy then
walked into the kitchen and asked me if he could come
over now. I just couldn't say no to the boy, and asked
him, "Have you had your breakfast?" He stood up
straight and said, "yes sir, and I made my bed, brushed
my teeth and said four Our Fathers' for you and your
family." I looked over at Sister Maria and she just
nodded her approval. I just smiled, looking down at
him, and said, "Let's go"!

I sat Jimmy down on an extra stool I sometimes used
as a table to eat my lunch. I was extra careful of his
burned legs, and his burned left hand that the sisters also
told me about. "Just be real careful," Sister Maria had
told me. He just smiled as he looked around my shop,
with the sunlight now coming through the dirty class
window panes. "How would you like to do me a favor?"
I asked. "Sure," he replied, then quickly added, "but I
can't do much!" I knew he wanted to do something, so I
said, "I noticed that you were coloring the other day at
the picnic table, and I was just wondering if you would
help me take inventory of what you see in my shop?
And then, if you want to; you can straighten up the paper
patterns and various designs in those boxes. And don't
rush, take your time; for while you're doing that you can
watch and see how I cut out these patterns on plywood.
That way, when you get better; I can teach you." His
eyes sparkled then, for I knew he wanted to learn. I

moved him closer to the other end of my work bench, where he could write and watch at the same time.

I reached into my scrap box and found a piece of plywood about ten inches long and six inches wide. Then I reached up and took a pattern from the top self, a cross. I showed the pattern to Jimmy and showed him where we needed to cut out the inside portions first and then outside lines of the cross last. Jimmy watched intently as I place the pattern on the plywood to see if it would fit. It did, so I turned the pattern over and with a brush from my pot of glue; I applied a very light coat of glue to the back of the pattern. Then I smooth the patter over the piece of plywood. I then laid the plywood down to dry.

"What's the next step," Jimmy asked, now watching me sitting there and not doing anything. "After the glue dries," I said, "it will be time to drill pilot holes into the wood. Each portion of the pattern that will be cut needs a pilot hole drilled so we can insert the saw blade into the hole and make the cut." I saw a puzzled look on his face, then I said, "Watch this Jimmy," and picked up my drill and chose a small cutout in the pattern, then I drilled my pilot hole. Then I picked up my saw, which I had already had the bottom portion of the blade attached to the handle with a turn screw. He watched closely as I inserted the top end of the saw blade through the pilot hole from the bottom side of the wood. Once through the pilot hole, I took the blade in my hand and fastened the top end of the blade to the upper end of the saw with a turn screw. Then I laid the plywood down flat on the end of my bench. Now with the pattern facing me, I moved the blade up and down…sawing very slowly along the pattern, ensuring that I stayed on the line. After the cut was complete, and the small wooden cutout fell to the floor; I loosen the top turn screw and removed the blade from the hole. Then I repeated the process and sawed another, and yet another cutout; having three tiny pieces of wood now on the floor.

"Kind of slow, isn't it?" Jimmy asked. "Well Jimmy," I said, "this is called Fretwork, it's the art of cutting our intricate patterns and designs in wood. And did you know, people have been doing Fretwork for over three thousand years!" He kept watching me then, not saying a word. Jimmy came back after lunch that day, stayed until evening meal time; then returned to the orphanage. I had finished the cross I was making and gave it to him. It wasn't anything fancy, just a simple cross with ivy leaves clinging to the cross from top to bottom. I had to make over sixty pilot holes for the internal cuts and the veining for the leaves. I asked him if he wanted to paint the cross, but he said no. I helped him as he placed the cross into a cloth bag and tied to bag to his crutches before he left.

Since that first day in my shop, Jimmy was hooked on working with his hands. I showed him how to cut a straight line, and even a perfect circle with my hand held saw. Jimmy came over almost every day now, except when it rained. But on those sunny mornings, he took some old newspaper and water and cleaned the glass windows of my shop. Then one morning he had noticed I had a lot of scrap wood in my wood box, wood that I would eventually throw away. He also noticed that I had several different patterns of a cross. Then one Sunday morning after church, he asked the question I knew he had on his mind.

"I was wondering," Jimmy said, "if you would make a cross for everyone's bed in the dormitory. "I was wondering when you were going to ask me that," I told him, then added, "Sister Maria had told me that you have already put your own up in your dorm, and now everyone wants one too." He looked sad just then, and for some reason I knew he wasn't being sad for himself; but for those who had no crosses over their bed. "Look," I said, "I have several here in this box." I counted out ten, of various sizes, and then looked up over the window frame…another six. That makes sixteen. Then Sister Maria was calling for Jimmy, and I helped him through the backyard.

Back inside my workshop, I recalled several years ago when I found a pattern book someone left on my doorstep…the same day at Mike delivered wood too, as I recalled. Well, I had gotten busy and cut out several and put them right…. here! I reached under my bench a pulled out a wooded box. Yep, another bunch of crosses, some finished; some not. I counted out seven that were complete. We now had twenty-three.!

The next morning when Jimmy hadn't arrived by nine o'clock, I took all twenty-three crosses over to Sister Maria. I also brought my small hammer and twenty-three small nails. The nails came from the wood pile outside my shop, still hammered into old boards. I pulled them out, some rusty and bent; but I straighten them out. Good enough for God's work, I told myself. The sister's helped me and before long we had all 23 crosses over each bed in the dorm, 24 if you count Toby's. Then Father Mathias arrived and went from bed to bed, blessing each and every one.

Jimmy continued coming over, and he started to make a cross from the scrap cutouts the accumulated on the floor. He asked me to make him a frame so he could place the pieces of wood inside. He worked on his cross every chance he got. But he also was to use the saw to make a portrait of a dog he had seen on one of my patterns. I gave him the pattern and watched as he carefully applied the glue on the back then attached the paper to the plywood. We waited for the glue to dry, then I made several pilot holes for him. I watched him as he held the saw's handle under him arm and used his good hand to thread the saw blade through the back side of the plywood. Then he put the saw's tubular arm under his arm and tightened the upper blade with the turn screw. He switched back to his good hand to make the cut. He wanted to use the drill, but his hand still hadn't healed enough to enable him to use the drill by himself.

The days went by quickly now, and soon turned into months; and still every afternoon after his classes Jimmy would knock on my door to see if it was okay to go into the shop an work on his project. I asked him one time what he was going to do with his project once it was finished. He already had the answer ready, "I'm going to sell it at the flea market. I want to have enough money to buy the sisters and Father Mathias new shoes. I already spoke with the man who sells shoes there, and he said that he would barter with me."

It was three days before Christmas when Maria came over to tell me that little Jimmy had passed. I hadn't seen him for a couple of days, and I had no idea he was ill. She told me that the funeral was going to be held in Nebraska where his parents are buried. I asked her if she was taking up a collection, and handed her a five dollar bill. She broke into tears and ran back to the orphanage. Somehow she knew that I wouldn't get another social security check until next week and that this was my last five dollars.

The following morning Father Mathias knocked on my door. He looked as if he had seen a ghost, his face was ashen, and he was trembling. He started to speak, then stopped…pointing to the bottle of brandy that was on my table. It was a Christmas present from my daughter. I poured the liquor into two small glasses, and no sooner had I finished; he picked a glass off the table and downed the brandy. Then he picked up the other glass and drank that too! "Please come with me," is all he said.

He led me over to the orphanage, and we went upstairs to the dormitory. Once inside the children's section saw several sisters were already there, now on their knees praying. I walked down the center of the dorm room, with beds on both sides, and over each bed I saw a cross that I had made. Father Mathias went over alongside one of the beds and removed a cross from the wall. He then walked next to me, and turned the cross over so I could see the back side. Then he handed it to me and I saw my name and the date I had completed making the cross, something that I have always done on the projects I made. I then looked around the room, and saw what Father Mathias was telling me; that all the crosses above each child's bed had turned into silver…including the one I was holding. I looked over at Jimmy's bed, and above the headboard was his cross, the one with ivy leaves…it had turned into gold!

I just stood there, not knowing what to say. "There's one more thing you need to also see," Father Mathias said. I followed him downstairs and into the chapel, and then up to the altar. There, shining brightly from the sun's rays coming through the skylight; was the cross that little Jimmy had made. It had taken him over two years to complete, a mosaic of small pieces of wood he had placed in such a manner that the no glue was used to hold the pieces together. The cross measured fourteen inches in length, and eight inches wide, and about one and a half inches thick. The cross had somehow transformed into gold, with blue and white diamonds encrusted on the bottom of the cross; so that it could stand up on its own. I looked closer now and could see that even though it was gold, you could still see the wood grain on each piece. Father Mathias went over and picked up the cross, and slowly turned it over on its back. Jimmy had followed my example by putting his name and date on the back. Then Father Mathias gave me a really puzzle look and said, "The date is the day little Jimmy passed…and it is in Jewish!"

Rafael

I had known Rafael a long time now, at least a year or so. I think that was the morning we were told to go to the headmistress together. We really weren't doing anything wrong, just playing football with a paper triangle; you know…kicking field goals with our fingers. I mean, it was lunch period after all. And it wasn't our fault when Rafael kicked the "ball" and it flew over my head and made a splash landing in Myrtle's soup bowl. We were in the 5th grade then, attending St. Basil's middle school up on the Vomero; a suburb overlooking the city of Naples. At the end of the school year, we were transferred to the Montessori school located in the crater at Agnano; just a few miles north of Naples. We had attended the 6th grade there, and in the fall will be attending the high school just a few blocks away. But this story isn't about the schools we attended, it's about Rafael and I accidentally discovering…

It was on a Thursday afternoon, and our graduating class was attending a field trip; a required 6th grade assignment that had been postponed several times. Finally, permission was granted for our class to visit the ruins at Baia, a small coastal village just north of Naples. I still think we could of have permission much earlier had they known our class consisted of five boys and five girls. Rafael, I call him Raf, and I had our backpacks ready: two cameras, four rolls of film, two water bottles, and band aids (Raf's mother's idea). I had my Dads flashlight and Raf had one he borrowed from his sister. We were ready!

Our teacher, Miss Maria, got us kids excited about the trip; showing us slides of ruins and telling us of such things as the Temples of Venus and Diana. She really got my interest when she mentioned the old port cities of Averno, Miseno, and Lucrino…even of several Roman baths. But when she said that the real entrance to the Gates of Hell was also located in Baia…our ears perked right up. Now, we thought…how cool is that!

It wasn't long after we had walked by the sign at read "Entra", picked up a map of the grounds, and took off. We didn't even give Miss Maria a chance to take another roll call. Heck, we had just graduated the 6th grade; we were men now and would be attending high school in the fall. Which meant, by the way; we were now "freshmen". We hid ourselves behind the Temple of Venus, out of Miss Maria's line of sight. The Temple of Diana wasn't on the grounds, to see that you had to cross the street. Then Raf saw where it was on the map that the temple was out of bounds due to extensive damage. "Oh well, so much for the gates to the netherworld," I said to Raf. Twenty minutes later we caught up to Miss Maria, or rather; she caught up to us. We stayed with the group for a while, then Raf said," You know Tommy, if the gates to hell were here; then there would be a huge sign showing us the entrance." "You're thinking what I am thinking," I said, then added, "we got to get across the street over to the Temple of Diana."

We checked the map again, and Raf pointed to the long walkway on the other side of the park. "Remember," he said, "that it ran down to what looked like a storage garage." "Worth checking out," I replied, and we took off running. I didn't know what was behind the door, but it had two padlocks with two sets of chains. We started to walk away when I thought of a trick my Dad had played on me more than once. He had an old locker down in our basement and kept it locked all the time. On morning I saw him close the locker and apparently hadn't noticed me on the stairs. He just wrapped the chain around both handles and placed the locked in front. Pretty clever, but now I knew. "Wait a minute Raf," I said, "let me try something." I walked up to the double doors and removed the chains from the door handles. The heavy chain slipped from my grip and down it went, locks and all.

It was dark inside the storage room and we got out our flashlights. The room went back further and we soon discovered that we were in a tunnel. Pieces of broken statues were lying everywhere. Vases of all sizes lined the walls as well as gardening equipment. We kept walking until we heard the cars on the road above us. Scared, we hurried across until we came to the other end of the tunnel. We opened the door, and there before us was the Temple of Diana. It really was in bad shape, with broken columns lying on the ground. And the garden, such as it was; was overflowing with weeds. The water in the pools along the foundation was stagnant and smelled foul. No wonder they kept this place off limits. And the area was really small too, about the size of our school gym. We decided to head back and walked around a fountain towards the tunnel when all of a sudden the ground under our feet gave way.

It was about a fifteen foot drop onto a sandy floor. We were alright, but Raf had broken the lens on his flashlight. The light bulb was broken too, he said. Good old Dad, I thought. He taught me quite a bit about flashlights and how to maintain them. I unscrewed the back of his old Navy issue flashlight and took out a new light bulb and three lenses: one yellow, one red, and one clear. We replaced the broken parts to Raf's flashlight and started to find out where we were. I thought of the passageways that Miss Maria had talked about in class, where the Romans used to walk through going back and forth from Lago d'Averno to Lago Lucrino. The passageway led in both directions and was damp and cold. And it was getting on to evening and Miss Maria would be pissed off if we didn't return soon. I looked at Raf and said, "This might be the passageway to hell, but we are going to be in a hell a lot sooner if we don't head back now." "Good thinking", Raf replied, then added, "we can come back later. And once we get back up, let's get our location fixed; we can probably get back inside here without going through the tunnel."

The following Saturday, we got up early; telling our parents we were going to Carney Park…our new code name for the Temple of Diana. We took the bus to Baia and got off at the stop across the street from the Temple of Diana. Even though it was only nine o'clock in the morning, a lot of tourists were shopping in the area; we had to squeeze our way through several old couples just to cross the street. But we were here, with the temple looming right above us.

The iron fence separating us from the temple grounds was too high to climb. And besides, there were too many people in the area who would probably call the police. We decided to walk along the fence, and then just at the end of the property; we saw a small trail leading around to the back. We had seen these trails before, made by school kids taking a short cut through the area. Soon we came to a small gate and as luck would have it, it was open. We walked through and stood next to the open hole in the ground we had made; apparently still unnoticed. Looking around and seeing no one, we threw our backpacks into the hole and jumped in after them. I overheard Raf mumbling a few words, and I think he said, "To Hell and Back," as we jumped.

The early morning sun lighted in the tunnel, or it seemed so; and when we broke out our map we found we didn't need any additional light. Last night we went over our planned venture into the underworld. We decided to take the eastward passage, because according to our map; would lead us directly towards Lago d'Averno. And that was the location our reference books said were where the gates to hell are supposed to be, not here in Baia. Both Raf and I weren't kids anymore, and since we were not kids; we weren't going to take any chances of getting turned around or lost. I took a large ball of heavy twine from my backpack. I removed the paper label saw on the label that the ball contained 1,000 feet of string. Raf also had a ball of twine in his backpack just in case. We fastened one end to a heavy piece of marble and tied three square knots so it wouldn't unravel when pulled on. I was anxious to get going, but Raf said to wait a minute. He then pulled up his pant leg and showed me his Mom's Pedometer that he had strapped to his ankle. He zeroed out the gauge and then said, "Let's go!"

About two hundred feet into the tunnel it became dark once again. We turned on our flashlights and now instead of seeing broken pieces of marble and garden equipment, there were crushed cans of Peroni and Nastro Azzuro beer; empty wine bottles too! Further down, Raf said we were only about three hundred feet or so and probably would have least another mile before we cleared the hillside overhead. Needless to say, we were starting to wonder if this as such as great idea in the first place when I saw what looked like an old Roman helmet. It turned out to be someone's old motorbike helmet that had a big crack on the side. Then Raf spotted something shinny along his side of the tunnel. It was a broken piece of glass and now I was also starting to get discouraged. "Let's pick up the pace," Raf said, and we started walking faster.

At the two thousand foot mark we found nothing but trash. And not just trash, but old trash at that; and it stunk! And at the 2,500 foot mark, we saw more of the same. But at the 3,000 foot mark we found an old spear. The wooden part of wormy and worn so we broke it off and the copper spearhead Raf put in this backpack. As we were nearing the 4,000 foot mark as indicated on Raf's pedometer, we began to see light coming from the other end of the tunnel. We were seeing more trash now too as we continued towards the end, and ten minutes later we arrived. The tunnel ended abruptly, and we were now looking out over the water of Lago d'Averno; the water level being about three feet below where we were standing. The lake smelled of sulfur, decaying fish, and rotten garbage. Raf pointed to the body of a dead animal with its entrails rotting away in the noonday sun. Then and there, we both lost our breakfast.

We made it back to the temple and across the street to catch the late afternoon bus heading back to Pozzuoli. Once in our seats, Raf took out the spear head we had found earlier in the tunnel and we got a better look at it in the sunlight. It looked old and we thought it was made of copper. Raf said his Dad would know for sure, so we put it back in his backpack. We went to my house first, dropped off my backpack, and headed over to Raf's place. He had invited me to dinner and I was looking forward to his Mom's spaghetti. It wasn't that my Mom wasn't a good cook, it's just that Raf's Mom is Italian; and her garlic bread....fantastic! His Dad collected all sorts of stuff, much of it from around Italy; and thought that the spear head was really unusual. He asked us if he couldn't take it to work with him tomorrow because at his library he would be able to find more information.

The next morning Raf came over to my house again to just hang out, sitting on our balcony; that just happened to have a real nice view of the amphitheater in Pozzuoli. I was looking at the tunnels that ran back and forth through the middle of the stadium and wondered it that would be worth exploring. "You checking on that girl downstairs?" Raf asked. "What girl?" I responded, because he definitely caught me by surprise and I sure did want to see a girl if there was any around. "Right down there," he said, and pointed to my sister; who was hanging clothes on our outside line. "Very funny," I replied and then we heard, "Hey guys, come over here." It was my Dad who was sitting next to Raf's Dad at our dining room table. "Check this out," my Dad said, then he pointed to a picture of a spearhead on the page of a book. It was exactly like the one we found. Raf and I just sat down.

Raf's Dad went on to explain, "The spearhead you boys found is old, really old. The shape of the spearhead is identical to the spearhead that once belonged to Spartacus. If you remember your history, Spartacus was a slave that escaped from Rome and eventually led a revolt against the Roman's. He was able to muster an army of over 70,000 slaves before eventually being overtaken in several battles by eight legions of Roman soldiers. It was told that in the end, Pompey took the last of Spartacus's army of 6,000 slaves and ordered them crucified along the Apian Way. Beginning at the village of Capua, and lining both sides of the roadway; the crosses ended at the very edge of the city of Rome. It was also told that Spartacus's body was never found."

"You're not going to tell us that this is his spear, are you?" Raf asked his Dad. "One thing for sure," he replied, "is that this is definitely a spear of that time period. And was apparently made for army officers, a solid gold spear with heavy copper plating for strength and weight. This spearhead is rare, very rare. I believe that book mentions that there are only two of them in existence: one at the Roman Museum of History in Rome and the other one in London. I'll have this checked out tomorrow through my office, and if I am right; you boys will definitely have your high school and college education paid for; with probably something left over."

"How cool is that," we both said in unison. Then it dawned on me, and I said, "You know Raf, we still have the other half of that tunnel to explore!" Both of our Dad's just looked at us....

St. Michaels

"Henry," my wife called, "Jenny is here to see you."
"Be there in a minute," I shouted as I pushed my
wheelchair and took off down the ramp that curved
around the stairway next to the dining room and ended
up in front foyer. Hank from next store built this for me
last year. It is the fastest way to go from upstairs to
downstairs, especially in the event of a crisis. "What's
up?" I asked Jenny as I came to a stop at the doorway.
Jenny was much bigger now, going on sixteen; or was it
seventeen. I had seen her every now and then at the
center but she hasn't been coming around lately.

I rolled my wheelchair up next to hers and said, "It's
has been a while young lady, I hope everything is well

with your family?" "Everything is okay," she answered, "except that I have been spending most of my time with my boyfriend down at the bowling alley. And watching him bowl made me remember what you had said about the center. That if we ever wanted to get involved in bowling that you and your friends had several ideas which could help us. "We still are involved," I responded, the said, "In fact, St. Michaels has sold their community center to my group. We were looking into that particular building because at one end it has a full size cafeteria which could easily be converted into a snack bar. The middle has been used for basketball games and the bleachers are still there, but we thought that perhaps we could remove those that are along one wall. And the far side of the building is large enough to install the machinery and electrical systems. And, if my engineer is correct in his estimates; we could have a professional bowling center with a total of sixteen lanes.

"But Henry," Jenny said, "That is why I don't bowl anymore. The Manager at the Lakeside Bowl said that I and other like myself with limited movement were causing the wooded boards on his lanes to weaken. He said he already had to replace them once and he is not about to do it again because it had cost him $24,000 dollars. So your building another bowling alley isn't going to help people like us."

"I understand completely," I said, "but let's go downstairs for a minute. I have something I want to show you. And let's take the elevator, it's much quicker." Once down in our basement, I turned on the overhead lights and Jenny gave out a loud gasp. "I have to give all the credit to Amy, for it was her idea," I said. Then I added, "It was almost completed when she died. There before her eyes, were two full size bowling lanes. I had started design changes right after I spoke with the kids at the center. I wanted to develop a way for kids to bowl and I believe I have finally found the solution. And with the help of Hank and Frank, we had engineered a brand new concept for bowling. Our modifications allows not only people in wheelchairs, but anyone who has difficulty with either picking up the heavy ball or trouble bending down to the floor to release the ball; while enjoying bowling."

"The only real change you see," I said, "that is different from any other bowling lane is that on the right of each lane I have installed a ramp that comes up just about two and a half feet. The ramp can be extended out about five feet from the lane itself. The top of the ramp is concave and has room for several bowling balls. The bowler removes his ball from the automatic ball return and places the ball on the ramp, then moves the ramp back and forth until reaching the foul line; which is perpendicular to the foul line below on the lane. It's kind of line a ball return, except in reverse."

I watched as Jenny gave the machine a kind of weird look, then said, "My technicians came up with several levers which are attached to the ramp which cause the ball to spiral, back spin, or curve to the right or left…just as would a bowler would normally. With practice, you would be able to control somewhat the action of the ball as it rolls down the lane; much like professionals." Then I asked her to move over next to me so she could get a better view of the ball launcher. "This is pretty neat, Henry," Jenny said, "but would it work on regular bowling lanes?" I had to smile at her then, she was a bright girl. "We've thought about that too," I said, "and the launcher can be removed in a matter of minutes, and without marring the surface of the wooded floors." She grinned and said, "Cool!"

On our way back upstairs, I told her that I was having a few members of the American Bowling Congress come by next Monday. Then I said to her, "If you would do me the honor, I would like you to be present. They would want to see firsthand how a person confined to a wheelchair would be able to move within the prescribed distances already sanctioned by the Congress." "They use measurements?" Jenny questioned. "Sure do," I replied, then said, "So I am asking you, would you like to spend a couple of days here learning the ins and outs of this contraption that Hank created." "Gladly," she responded then said, "I can't wait. The only difference I can see right now is that I would be sitting back while pushing the ball forward. And we would be under the same association regulatory rules. And, we would not have to spend hours trying to find a bowling ball, we wouldn't need to put our fingers into any holes."

That was on Wednesday, and by Saturday Jenny had bowled over twenty games. She was bursting with joy because her fingers didn't hurt, she didn't need the holes to hold onto the ball. And she had managed to learn to curve a ball, as I watched her ball leaving the ramp. Naturally, her moments were slower; but I continued to watch as her ball headed for the second arrow on the lane she had aimed for. Once past the arrow, the ball curved to the left and struck the right side of the head pin... a strike! Then she showed me her backspin next, successfully completely a 5-6 split for a spare. She was having fun, and excitingly said, "You just got to watch my power ball!" She started at the end of the ramp and pushed the ball hard, ensuring that her hand did not go past the foul line. I watched as her ball sped down the ramp, spiraling in a left to right motion; then striking the head pin just to the left. She left the 7-9 pins standing. On her attempt to convert to a spare, she hit the 9 pin head on and left the 7 pin standing. "Think this will catch on?" asked. "You bet," she said and so did my wife; who had been watching all along.

It was opening day at St. Michael's Bowling Center, and I was quite surprised to see a crowd beginning to form at the entrance. The ABC sanctioned our bowling alley and soon thereafter three other parishes joined, each forming three leagues. Much thought had gone into our league formation and little Jenny's experience from hanging around bowling alleys proved useful. In addition, she grew up knowing exactly what her limitations were imposed on her and her wheelchair. In short, she knew exactly how many chairs would accommodate a lane during league play. So the teams were limited to four players on each team, with each league allowing up to six teams. Only two teams per league were allowed during a single meet or tournament.

St. Basil's arrived with two teams as well as St. Mathews. From Pittsburgh came St. Andrews with two teams, and all wore Irish green bowling shirts. St. Michaels, well; Jenny was nominated Captain of her team. The center choose their colors: White with Red/Blue trim. I voted against having sponsors for St. Michaels on the back of their bowling shirts. And, since I was footing the bill, I got my way. Although I did permit player numbers, and they came up with a single white patch with a red number; and red/blue trim...and it looked great!

I didn't have a doubt that St. Michaels would win their first tournament. We even built a display case next to the snack bar so all could see view our accomplishments. To this day, no one has ever bowled a perfect game using the assisted bowling ramp; but Jenny came close... with a 263. Other parishes have started to come by our bowling center to see what the commotion was all about. We even made a film, and I made Jenny a "star". I also talked with Jim Fowler the other day and he informed me that the ABC has authorized two professional league of "assisted bowling." Bowling alleys throughout the country are now installing at least four assisted bowling lanes in their establishments. And it is my understanding that if an individual can meet the point requirements of professional bowlers, he or she can participate. The sport has come a long ways. For it has become apparent that many women and children who used to dread the heavy balls, having to hold onto them with only their fingers; can easily just push the ball down onto the lane. To that end, St. Michaels is now hosting a 65+ bowling tournament next week.

Our pastor, Father Givens; called me this morning to attend a meeting at his rectory. It seems that several members of our parish wanted to discuss the bowling center with me. I asked Jose to take me over in his van if he wasn't too busy. He just laughed and said, "After all you have done, they should send a limo for you." Then he just shook his head and said, "Let's go, we're burning daylight!" He must have had watched a John Wayne movie last night, I thought to myself.

We arrived at the rectory and Jose and I entered the library. There were six members of the parish in attendance, and I happened to notice that all but one were women, but didn't think anything of it. Then Father Given's rose from his chair and explained that several members were requiring as to the distribution of funds that we receive. Jose' started to giggle, then burst out laughing. I gave him a stern look and he excused himself and left the room. "I'm sorry Father," I said, then asked, "What funds are we referring too?"

One woman from the opposite end of the table said, "Well, what about profits from the Snack Bar?" I pulled out my notebook, then replied, "Our last quarter's profit was a negative $35,000.00." "How could that be," she shot quickly back at me. "Well," I started to explain, "That is probably because none of you have ever seen a cash register in the Snack Bar. Nor, will there ever be one as long as the building belongs to me. You see, only children in wheelchairs and their guests are allowed to eat there and they do not pay. I run the Snack Bar as a tax write off and will continue to do so. "What about the bowling fees?" another well intentioned lady asked. I smiled and said, "The Pro Shop also has no cash register so that should tell you that what applies to the Snack Bar also applies to the Pro Shop."

I paused a moment, then looked directly at each person at the table and said, "I hope that my intentions are not being misunderstood just because I am a millionaire and I have unlimited resources. I sponsor a community center for those confined to wheelchairs, such as myself; regardless of race or religion. I also sponsor a bowling center, and again, regardless to race or religion. The children who frequent my centers are extremely excited about their opportunity to enjoy activities they normally would be shunned from. And, the only participation requirement is a grade C average; and we do check. By the way Father, how many children do you have attending your parish school who have below a C average?" "Thanks to you sir," Father Givens replied, "None!" Then the good father rose as the ladies left the room, with a big Irish grin on his face!

Printed in Great Britain
by Amazon

22288974R00106